Journey
of the
Sparrows

to María Elena, Barbara,
Margaret, and Miriam

PUFFIN BOOKS
Published by the Penguin Group
Penguin Putnam Books for Young Readers,
345 Hudson Street, New York, New York 10014, U.S.A.
Penguin Books Ltd, 80 Strand, London WC2R ORL, England
Penguin Books Australia Ltd, Ringwood, Victoria, Australia
Penguin Books Canada Ltd, 10 Alcorn Avenue, Toronto, Ontario, Canada M4V 3B2
Penguin Books (N.Z.) Ltd, 182-190 Wairau Road, Auckland 10, New Zealand

Penguin Books Ltd, Registered Offices: Harmondsworth, Middlesex, England

First published in the United States of America by Dutton Children's Books,
a division of Penguin Books USA Inc., 1991
Published by Puffin Books, a division of Penguin Putnam Books for Young Readers, 2002

7 9 10 8 6

THE LIBRARY OF CONGRESS HAS CATALOGED THE DUTTON EDITION AS FOLLOWS:
Buss, Fran Leeper, date.
Journey of the sparrows / by Fran Leeper Buss with the assistance of Daisy Cubias.—1st ed.
155 p. ; 22 cm.
Summary: Maria and her brother and sister, Salvadoran refugees, are
smuggled into the United States in crates and try to eke out a living
in Chicago with the help of a sympathetic family.
ISBN: 0-525-67362-8 (hc)
[1. Salvadorans—United States—Fiction. 2. Illegal aliens—Fiction.]
I. Title.
PZ7.B9655 Jo 1991 [fic]—20

Puffin Books ISBN 0-14-230209-0

Printed in the United States of America

Journey
of the
Sparrows

FRAN LEEPER BUSS

WITH THE ASSISTANCE OF DAISY CUBIAS

PUFFIN BOOKS

CHAPTER ONE

My sister, brother, and I were pressed together in the dark crate. I felt the body of the fourth person, the boy Tomás, tight against me as we all held our breath and lay without moving. "Immigration, *la migra*. Be still!" warned the man who was smuggling us north. Breathing in the crate had been hard before, and feeling faint, I'd tried to gulp the air. But now I was afraid to breathe at all. Oscar, my six-year-old brother, began to whimper, and my big sister, Julia, clamped her hand across his mouth and pulled him tighter on top of us. I could feel Tomás begin to shake against my back, and I was pressed so tightly against Julia's swollen stomach that I thought I felt the baby move.

There was a muffled crying outside, perhaps from another crate, then silence, filled only by the smells of onions and tomatoes. Suddenly, the sacks and boxes of vegetables on top of our crates were banged around, and a man shouted out orders in English I couldn't understand. His voice sounded cruel, like the voices of the government soldiers, the Guardias, who had come to our home months before.

I felt tears run down my face, but I couldn't get a hand

free to wipe them. Julia's shoulders rocked back and forth as she pressed Oscar's face into her chest, and the pain in my bent neck spread to my head and across my shoulders. Finally, the men's voices moved farther away, and the engine of the truck in which we were hidden started up again. Then the familiar voice of the man shouted in Spanish, "They're gone. It's clear."

It had been dark when we were nailed into the crate, but now a crack let in a line of light from the day. The crate clattered on the floor of the truck, our bodies vibrated against one another, and the engine roared continually. Julia was to my left, and Tomás, to my right. He was bent and lying on his side, his chest behind my hips and his legs bent under my legs. I was sitting now, trying to curl forward, my knees up and over his legs. With each jerk of the truck, I felt thrust tighter against this strange boy's body. I could feel his warmth and moisture, and his sweat smelled salty. Little Oscar squirmed across Julia and me, none of his body touching the bottom of the crate. As time passed, the pain curved slowly down my spine until my back felt as if it were breaking.

Finally, I couldn't stand it one more minute. I jerked my chest forward against my legs, desperate to straighten myself out, and knocked Julia hard against the crate. Oscar fell down, around our legs.

"Julia, María, let me out!" Oscar cried, thrashing. "I'm thirsty. I want Mamá." He pounded the crate with his hands.

I sobbed out loud. "I'm sorry, Julia. I'm sorry." Terror rose up inside me.

"Our Father," Tomás began to pray behind me.

I felt Julia grope in the near dark for Oscar's hands and, restraining them, she said sternly, "María, calm down. We'll make it. Calm down. Try to breathe slowly."

I curled my back again and attempted to do as my sister told me.

2

Julia twisted around until she was balanced again, then whispered more gently, "Little Sister, it'll help to remember good things. Remember the *amate* tree at home."

"Yes," I said, struggling to sound calm.

"Remember how I pushed you up into the tree, before you were old enough to climb on your own?"

I nodded in the dark.

"Remember how Papá would sit against it at night, after they came back from the fields?"

"Yes. Papá," I answered.

"Papá," Oscar echoed.

"Remember the songs he used to sing?" Julia began to sing quietly, her voice strained:

> "Tender little birds
> That sing at dawn,
> Trees dressed up
> In emerald green."

I turned my head away. I didn't want to think about Papá or Julia's husband, Ramón. They were gone. Then Julia began to sing a love song, one of the ones we'd sung when Julia and Ramón were married. Her singing seemed to calm Oscar.

I tried to think of my home. The sky, think of the sky, I told myself. I squeezed my eyes shut, despite the darkness in the crate, and tried to see the colors. The piercing blue of the sky, always with me, seemed to pull me upward, and I felt it touch my cheeks and calm my face, like my mother's hand on me when I was younger. Then I saw our land during the rainy season. The world was green, and immense white clouds shared with me their secret faces of the saints. Flocks of green and yellow parakeets soared over our heads, and in October, light pink coffee blossoms whispered their sweet smell into the clear air. Our brown-and-white rooster crowed at dawn each

3

day, and in the evenings, sunsets wove the clothes of the Indians from Papá's stories, using yarns of red, gold, violet, and blue. Inside the church, the blue robes, yellow flowers, and the holy faces of the Virgin and the saints gave us courage, and in the tower, the bell rang out the rhythm of our lives and tolled the death of my brothers and sister.

All this I thought of while I was curled in the crate. We'd been so poor at home. Just flowers and hunger. Four brothers and one sister died from worms and lack of food. Finally, Papá and a few others brought a nurse and a teacher into our village, and that's how I learned to read. I imagined my teacher, standing by the chickens in front of her little house. Her left hand was on her hip; her right hand was pulling back her long hair as she watched the sunset. But the red of the sunset began to spread outward, toward me, flowing as though bleeding, and I heard the clicks as the guns went into position, and I saw people, their mouths open, screaming.

I jerked my head back and forth, back and forth in the crate, trying not to remember. "Quetzal!" I suddenly cried out loud. "Quetzal! Quetzal! Help us! Help us!" I pounded the crate above my head with my fists, sobbing, until Julia twisted her body and tried to grab my arms.

Tomás jerked up from his side and grabbed me from behind, holding my back against his chest and trying to pull my hands down. "Stop," he yelled. "Be calm." Slowly, I quit fighting so hard and leaned my forehead against my knees, crying. I pictured the quetzal bird.

"María," Julia said again with sternness. "We must not break down. Now tell me. Tell me the story of how you found the quetzal. It'll help you feel better."

My voice shook, but I tried to do as she told me. "We'd been traveling down a path in the mountains, and that's where we were when we came upon a stack of small cages."

"That's right. Who got there first?"

4

"I did. But Oscar was right behind me." I stopped speaking, still crying quietly.

"Go on," Julia ordered.

"There was a big green bird. It was thrashing around in the bottom cage. I got down on my knees and looked inside. That's when you came. I told you it would die."

"Yes, that's how it went. What did I say?"

"You said that the trappers were probably close by. That we should hide."

"Then what happened?"

"Mamá arrived also. She said, 'A quetzal, like in your papá's stories.' You asked Mama, 'Really, the good quetzal?' Mamá said yes. Oscar said, 'It's magic.' "

Tomás let go of me and spoke from behind me in the dark. "You mean you really found a quetzal?"

"Yes, we did," Julia said. "It was when we were wandering through the mountains." I could feel her turn toward him. Only now did I realize how tightly Tomás had been holding me. My body burned with shame. What would my mother or grandmother say about a girl who sat this close to a boy? I was grateful Julia couldn't see my skin redden in the dark.

"Go on, Little Sister. What did you do then?"

"I twisted the wire that held the cage closed. The bird was scared, and its wings thrashed even harder. Then the wire jerked in my fingers, and the door sprang open."

"And we all jumped back," Julia continued.

"Me too. I remember," Oscar added, as he squirmed into a different position.

"The bird flopped out of the cage," I said, looking around my arm in Tomás's direction. I couldn't see his face in the dark. "At first its wings wouldn't work, but then it rose up past us into the sky. Its long tail spread behind it, and we could see its other colors."

Then I whispered to myself the end of our story:

5

" 'Quetzal!' I called, as it flew away. 'Help us. Help us make it to safety.' "

Our truck hit a bump in the road, and the crates bounced up and crashed down. My head smashed against the top of the crate, my neck hurt even more, and my hips ached. We heard screams from the crates around us, and Oscar wet himself against my legs. He cried and cried, and I tried to pat and soothe him. Julia was also crying, and Tomás was praying again.

As Oscar's urine became cold, I realized how icy the whole crate was becoming. Tomás shivered and Oscar complained, "I'm cold. I'm thirsty."

Oscar cried softly as hours went by. Then all at once, Julia shouted, "I can't see the light! It's gone. I'm blind! I'm blind!"

I was confused and terrified. I must have fallen asleep. "No," Tomás said to Julia. "You're not blind."

"It's the night," I cried urgently. "Julia, it's probably the night. I can't see the light either."

Tomás shook, and I felt the cold work its way up my spine and down my arms. My legs felt numb and asleep, but my knees ached.

"I'm so thirsty," Julia said.

"What's wrong with me?" Tomás groaned. "Why didn't I bring any water?"

"Home," Julia moaned. "Ramón, I want to go home." Then in panic, "María, where are you?"

"I'm here, Julia. I won't leave you."

"What about my baby? It's not moving. What if this has killed Ramón's baby?"

"Your baby's alive. I felt it move when *la migra* stopped the truck." I tried to keep talking, but I was so thirsty, my swollen tongue stuck to the roof of my mouth. My words were blurred, and my throat ached from wanting water.

6

We huddled in silence for awhile, shaking with the cold. Oscar kept moaning, "Water." I repeated the rosary, "Pray for us sinners . . . at the hour of our death . . . Mother of God . . ." and could no longer tell if I was crying or if it was one of the others. I didn't sleep anymore, but my mind drifted away, and once I thought I felt green-feathered wings brush against my face. I was back at the river where we crossed, and I heard the deep churning sounds of the water and the steady call of frogs.

Tomás began to shout, breaking into my thoughts. "My foot! I can't move my foot. It's frozen!" He jerked frantically against me, flinging his arms against my back.

"Stop, Tomás. Stop!" I screamed.

He stopped swinging his arms and started to cry. "It's the cold and these boots," he sobbed. "These damn small boots. They've cut off the blood to my feet. Oh God, it wasn't this bad when I came before."

I groped in the dark, trying to rub his foot, thinking, You've come before? You lived through it? You're alive? I felt his wet face against my back. His tears were warm.

The cold seemed to wrap itself around me and pulled me into myself until I felt far away from the others. Finally, I no longer moved or thought but lay silently against the other bodies.

Then, from far away, I heard banging on the crates. Our crate jolted and something tore against the wood. I blinked. A bright light glared in on us, and I could move my head backward. A man grabbed my arm and yanked me upward, saying, "Come on. Get out. Get out!" Staring into the light, I felt exposed, as if I had nothing on. I stumbled up, out of the crate, then collapsed down among other bodies in the back of the truck. I lay there in the dark until Oscar began to cry.

Soon the men who had brought us pulled us down off the truck and herded us out of the night into a building.

7

Julia and I stood huddled together in the bright light. Oscar was in my arms, still whimpering. His brown eyes were rolled to the side, and we couldn't make him stand up.

A dark-haired woman stepped toward us, touched Julia's arm, and said in our language, "I have come for Tomás. May they burn in hell for how they brought you. Wrap the boy in my coat and come with me."

We followed her without speaking. She led us outside, into another building, up many steps, and finally into a room with heat, where she gave us water and aspirin and told us to rest on the floor. Staring into the glowing wires of a small heater, I fell asleep, and in my dreams I hurled myself at the men, pounding them with my fists as they nailed us into the crate. Then I blushed, realizing I was pressed against Tomás's body.

I woke up suddenly, confused, and looked from the heater into the face of an old woman dressed all in black. The woman's dark eyes peered at me from her wrinkled face. Bits of white hair had pulled out from her bun, and she smelled of herbs, like a midwife. "You are awake. Here, drink water," she said. "How you all have suffered."

The water was cool as I swallowed it, and the warmth of the room was gentle. *"Gracias,"* I said to the old woman as I put down the empty cup. I was still on the floor, and Julia lay sleeping next to me, her face finally peaceful. Oscar slept on a couch. He was drawn and pale, and one arm covered his eyes. Tomás sat awake on the floor, fingering the handle of an empty cup. He rested with his back against a cracked wall, and his left foot was wrapped in bandages. He'd been pushed behind me into the crate when it was dark, before I'd seen him. Now I saw that his face was broad and still, with dark circles beneath his eyes, which were looking downward. He was not yet a grown man, perhaps fifteen, my age, or a few years older. Across the room, the light of

8

a candle flickered in front of a statue of San Antonio, and the saint stared at me with solemn, knowing eyes. I smelled incense and herbs, like in our church at home, and heard voices and a child crying somewhere.

The woman who had led us here knelt down by me, held some coffee to my lips, and pushed my long hair back from my face. "I'm Marta, Tomás's aunt, and this is Doña Elena," she said, motioning to the old woman kneeling next to her. "She came to help you. The little boy is sleeping now. And your sister's baby is alive. She won't lose it." Her eyes filled with tears. "But Tomás's foot is frozen. Doña Elena is trying to save it."

Marta handed me the hot coffee and took another cup to Tomás. He looked over at us, and I pressed my dress down around my knees. Marta said, "What a long way you've had to come. You're from El Salvador, aren't you?"

I jerked up and my face burned, I was so frightened. If they knew, they might send us home. I shook my head violently.

But the woman just stared at me and nodded. "Yes, you are," she said gently. "Yes."

Finally, I whispered, "We can't go back. They'll kill us. We're here and Mamá and Teresa are sick, down in Mexico. Please don't send us back."

The old woman answered from my other side. "No, my child. Don't be afraid. We won't hurt you."

CHAPTER TWO

I fell asleep again and dreamed, and in my dream the wind picked me up so I sailed through the air, stretching my arms and legs as far as they could reach. Then the wind swept me home to my village and set me down gently outside our house of clay and sticks. I stood in the doorway, looking at the dark coolness inside, and heard my mother patting tortillas and singing to herself as she rocked Teresa:

> "The day when you were born
> All the flowers were born too.
> The day when you were born,
> The nightingales sang."

I heard laughter and turned to see Julia and me as young girls. We sat, giggling and shucking corn on burlap bags under our shed of sticks. Julia's legs were spread and her bare feet pressed into mounds of noontime dust, but she kept her face and shoulders in the shadows. Even so, her forehead and upper lip were wet with sweat as she worked. I sat farther in the shadows of the shed,

10

rubbing corncobs together and listening to Julia talk about Ramón. Julia's eyes, like mine, were as dark as coffee, but she had no dimple in her chin, and her skin was pale, like a light brown dove. I saw her reach out with an ear of corn as she laughed, and I followed the movement of her arm. But then I glanced down at my darker arms and legs, and I frowned.

Julia noticed my frown. "María," she said, "you're growing up. Boys'll notice you soon. See, I'll show you how big you are. Hold your hands up against mine." So we pressed our damp hands together in the coolness of the shed, but the difference in color was the difference between the sun and shadows, and I turned my face away from my sister.

When I woke up, it was morning. I squinted into the sun that streamed in through a cracked, lace-curtained window. The light was so bright after the darkness of the crate that I felt tears in my eyes. My whole body ached, and I groaned when I moved. My arms and legs were bruised and swollen, and my hands were raw from banging on the crate. I was still on the floor, covered with a blanket, but now only Tomás was near me. He lay in the same place he'd sat the night before and moaned in his sleep. I could hear Mexican music from another room.

My eyes adjusted to the light as I looked around. The room seemed bright with colors. One wall was a sharp yellow; the others were white. A picture with orange daisies hung to the left of the window, and a cross with large plastic purple and pink flowers—those put on graves in Mexico—was fastened to the wall on the right. A big poster of a red-headed woman, laughing and holding a glass of beer, hung above the couch. The words ME GUSTA CARTA BLANCA were written on it. Chains of gold and silver foil hung from one ceiling corner to another, and I thought of Christmas decorations I'd seen in a store.

11

Then I saw the television. It was turned off, but I'd never been so close to one before. I stood up, aching as I did, walked to the television, and gently swept my fingers across the smooth screen. The statue of San Antonio was placed carefully on a blue towel on top of the television, and a calendar with a blond Jesus holding a sheep was hung above it. As I reached out to touch the saint, Marta appeared in the doorway and motioned me to join her.

I stepped into a kitchen and saw Julia sitting on a chair. She held Oscar on her lap against her pregnant stomach. Our Lady, I thought to myself, you've brought us here alive.

Marta, a short, plump woman, was dressed as brightly as the colors in her home. "Oh, *mijita*," she said to me in her big, hearty voice as she examined one of my bruised arms, then the other. "Damn *coyotes*, they treated you so bad it'd make the Blessed Virgin swear! Outrageous. Outrageous." She clicked her tongue and shook her head, her chest jiggling with the motion. Julia and Oscar were also bruised and battered. Marta sat back down, and two little girls, their faces round like Marta's, came to stand partly behind her.

Images of saints, bright plastic flowers, and a poster of puppies with huge eyes were thumbtacked to the cracked yellow walls of the kitchen. A light bulb hung from the ceiling, a bag of potatoes lay in a cardboard box on the floor, and water from a faucet trickled into a sink. The radio playing music was on the counter, and a half-empty bread bag lay open on the table. My stomach jerked with hunger.

Julia lifted a cup of water to Oscar's lips and looked at me. Her voice was fearful. "Oscar can't talk," she said to me, "and his eyes keep rolling."

I bent down to Oscar, patted him on the face, and

12

shook his arm. "Oscar! Oscar! Little Sparrow. Look at me. It's María."

Oscar glanced in my direction; then his eyes rolled up and to the right. The pain that was already in my chest grew tighter. "How long has he been like this?" I asked Julia.

"When I was up during the night, he seemed better, but since he woke up this morning, his eyes have been rolling and he won't talk."

Marta sighed. She wore a low-cut blouse, and she reached in her bra and pulled out a handkerchief. She wiped the hanky across her forehead. "So many kids get hurt like that. Holy cats!" Suddenly, she threw up her hands and her voice became high pitched. "One of my nephews died along the way! People try so hard, you'd think this was the land of cream and honey. Tomás made the crossing once before, and we didn't hear about him for nine days." She reached across the table and felt Oscar's face. "How was Oscar before you left Mexico?"

"He was weak from not eating, but not like this," Julia answered.

"Oscar's very smart," I said. "When we were still home, I was teaching him how to read."

"*Pobrecito, pobrecito,* poor boy," Marta said, patting Oscar's hand. "Doña Elena'll try to help you." She nodded toward an empty chair. "Here, María, sit down and have some coffee and bread." I sat and bolted down the bread she handed me, its sweetness relieving my hunger. Then I looked at Oscar.

He was wearing underpants stained brown and a shirt without buttons; he seemed so small on Julia's lap. His bruised legs were spindly and his knees were swollen, like a child with worms. I thought of the way he used to balance mostly on one foot, his eyes wide and blinking when he seemed to be thinking of something special. I

13

had looked after him at home. He was always with me, talking all the time and following me in and out of the house, to the cornfields and to the well, usually trying to carry more rocks than his hands would hold. One time he found a sparrow with a broken leg. I helped him nurse the sparrow, and for some days, he'd carried the bird in one hand, little stones in the other. I called him "little Oscar Sparrow."

Marta pulled her red scarf off her short black hair and said, "I've been here four years this time. Left five kids in Mexico with my mother. My husband was here, and I came to be with him. But after we had two more girls, Immigration caught him and sent him back. When they took him, I hollered and screamed. Honest to God, I miss him." She set her coffee cup back onto the table and picked up one of her daughters. "Miss my kids in Mexico too. They're sick. That's why I have to stay here and work."

"Do you earn enough to help them?" Julia asked.

"A little, a little," Marta responded, shaking her flowing clothes.

I sat at the table, watching Julia, Marta, and Oscar, who seemed so sick and strange. Papá, I don't know if I can do it, I said to myself.

"We had a friend named Beatriz in Mexico," Julia said to Marta. "She told us how we would have to live, way up north like this. She said we'd have to be invisible, never complain, never get anybody to notice us. Because we wouldn't have papers. If they caught us, they'd send us back home."

Marta nodded.

I remembered Beatriz. We'd sat on the floor of her little adobe house as she ground red chilies and onions. Pale blue, smoky light sifted into the dark room through the

14

open door. Outside, a dog barked and a man was singing. My baby sister Teresa cooed on Mamá's lap.

"Some try to cross the border secretly. But lots drown," Beatriz had said. "I know people who crossed through the mountains, but they were caught and sent to jail. When I was young, before my kids, I walked through the desert, but it was terrible."

She set the chilies down and worked on dough for tortillas. "We found two bodies as we walked north," she said. "So we put crosses of sticks by their heads. I think rattlesnakes might have killed them." She dropped her hands to her lap. "Oh, how we suffer to get up there, where we're not even wanted, except to do work that others wouldn't do."

"But if we go home, we'll be killed. If we stay in Mexico, we'll starve. If we don't go north, we'll die," Julia whispered.

"Yes," Beatriz answered, "you'll die."

Now we were in Chicago, alive, hoping to send some money to Mamá and Teresa. We had finally paid *coyotes*, men who smuggle people, to bring us in the crates. I shuddered, thinking of the crates, and glanced at Oscar. Then I looked at Julia's face. It still held its beauty, with her almond-shaped eyes and the fullness of her upper lip, but her cheeks and lips were pale. The circles beneath her eyes had darkened, her hair had pulled out of the braid she wore down her back, and her stomach bulged unbelievably.

"You can stay with us until tomorrow," Marta said, "but you'll have to leave then. I've got lots of boarders. If only it wasn't winter." She started to chuckle, and clapped her hands on the table. "It's so cold, milk from a cow'd freeze before it hit the bucket." Julia smiled.

I went to the window. Even with the window closed,

the cold air struck my face, and I trembled when I saw how high we were. I blinked and looked down again. Other buildings surrounded us, and snow lay on the ground and on the roofs of the other buildings. People wrapped in coats walked with their heads bent down, and I saw no green, just a tree with no leaves that shook in the wind. Cars, more than I had ever imagined, made slushing sounds as they passed each other, and a bus pulled to a stop and splattered gray, wet snow on the street. A man was huddled against the building next to ours and didn't move like the other people. I watched him until a pigeon flew down onto a wooden landing across from us.

I smiled because the pigeon reminded me of the quetzal and of the birds at home. I looked back down on the man. He held a bottle but didn't drink from it, and I wondered how anyone could stand so quietly in such cold. Suddenly, I thought, Could he have followed us? Does he know we're here? I felt dizzy, stepped back away from the window, and sat down at the table, looking at Oscar. His eyes were closed now.

Julia sat quietly, and Marta poured her more coffee. "Do you have any money?" she asked gently.

Julia took a deep breath and said, "No, but I have this." She reached into the neck of her dress and pulled out the string with a little pouch.

I moved quickly to block her hand, we had hidden it so long. "Julia. No," I said. "Don't tell."

"Yes, María," she said to me and pushed my hand away. "I think it's time, and we have to trust somebody."

I glanced quickly at Marta and felt color leave my face. Shame burned along the lines of my cheeks, and I stared at the table.

Marta put her plump hand on mine. "It's okay, *mijita,*" she said. "I understand."

Julia shifted Oscar in her arms, pulled the string off her neck, and opened the pouch. She held the gold chain in her hand. Its color was like sunshine. "Mamá bought this for me when I was a little girl," Julia said, "for protection."

Marta bent over it. "Well, it'll probably buy you a place to sleep and food for a few days." She glanced down at her own hand. "I had a wedding ring once, but it's gone now." Tears came to her eyes. She took her hanky back out of her bra and blew her nose loudly. "We'll leave the kids here, get you some clothes from the church, and sell the chain. Tomorrow I'll take you all to some other Salvadorans."

Marta gave Julia two sweaters and a jacket to wear, and they went to the apartment door. "Julia," I whispered, "be careful. I think there's a man outside. I saw him leaning against the next building. He wasn't moving." Julia looked over at Marta, fears and questions in her eyes.

Marta went to the kitchen window and stared down at the street. "There's no one there now," she said. "It was probably just someone who's homeless. Life here isn't all fresh coffee and sugar."

Her daughters cried when she and Julia left. The younger reminded me of Teresa, my little sister still in Mexico. I stooped down and held her a minute, then handed her a bottle.

Oscar sat on a wooden chair, his eyes rolled up and unfocused, a blanket wrapped around him so only a bit of his face showed. Taking a piece of bread, I said, "Little Sparrow, eat for me." I put a bit against his mouth, and he stared at me and slowly chewed and swallowed it. I fed him a whole slice that way, talking to him as he ate it.

"Oscar," I said, "we made it. We're here in the North,

17

where everyone gets so rich. We'll have lots to eat, and we'll send money so Mamá and Teresa can join us. Mamá'll be here soon, I promise." His eyes widened. "And, Oscar, you can see down to the street from here. All the people have big coats, even the children. There's snow. When we get some clothes, we'll play in it."

I pointed to the window. "When it's cold like this, you can breathe against the glass so it fogs." I blew on it until it clouded and wrote Oscar's name with my finger. He watched me for a moment, one eyebrow slightly raised; then his eyes seemed to go blank. I tipped his face up toward me and went to the sink.

"See, Oscar," I said, "there's running water." I turned the faucet off and on as he watched me. "I think there's electricity too." I went to a switch on the wall and flicked it up and down several times. The light bulb lit up and went off as I did it. I began to smile, then laugh with pleasure, as I flicked it more quickly and glanced down at Oscar. His eyes blinked up at the ceiling with excitement.

"And I'm going to get some fancy high heels," I said to Oscar. "This is how I'll walk." I tiptoed around the room, fluttering my arms with elegance. "I'm going to be a special, high-class lady." Oscar smiled.

"There's even a television!" I went and held his hands. "Maybe when Marta gets home, she'll let us watch it." Oscar smiled wider. "See, Oscar. See how much hope there is."

Then I remembered the man outside. Maybe he'd noticed the light blinking off and on. I hurried to the window, flattening my back against the wall as I stared outside, over my shoulder. The man had come back to the building next door and was looking up in our direction. I felt sweat roll down my face. Oscar whispered, "María."

I moved away from the window, down to his level so his eyes met mine. "María," he said. "Papá says the shadow man is coming."

Tears filled my eyes, and I bent his head against mine. "Oh, Oscar, you're okay. Papá, Mamá," I cried. "What am I going to do?"

We sat still until I heard movement and looked up. Tomás stood on his right foot in the kitchen doorway. I lowered my eyes.

"I hope I didn't hurt you in the crate," he said. "When I couldn't move my feet. I'm . . . I'm ashamed, about how I acted."

I shook my head and blushed deeply, turning my face away. I remembered the pressure of his body as we were pushed together. "How's your foot?" I whispered.

"It hurts real bad. How's he?" He nodded toward Oscar.

I shook my head. "Not good."

Tomás hopped over toward the window. I continued to look away. "I hate it when it's cold up here," he said. "This trip was worse than before."

I glanced up at him while he was looking out the window. In the daylight I saw that his hair was brown and curly and fell over his forehead, not black, straight hair, like mine. Then I thought of the man outside. I opened my mouth to warn him, but no words came out.

Tomás turned toward me before I could drop my face. For an instant, I saw his eyes. They were blue, like our sky at home. I trembled, I was so embarrassed, but I felt the touch of the blue, like light on my face. Why does he have blue eyes? I wondered. His skin was nearly as dark as mine.

Tomás kept speaking as he limped to the sink. "Where we lived, when I was little, it was never cold like this. Just during the rains, it was sort of cold, and when I'd swim way out into the water. But the sun was warm, even in the water."

I didn't know what to say. I'd never been alone like this with a boy before, so I waited silently for Julia and Marta to return. I checked the window twice, but the man was gone. Finally, I heard a noise outside the door, and Marta came blustering in, followed by Julia. They were carrying clothes. I felt tears of relief in my eyes. Marta looked over at me and said, "That man, the one you were afraid of, no problem. He's just a bum."

Later, Marta turned on the television, and we sat staring at it, our mouths open, as we watched a program called "Popeye the Sailor Man." Cartoon drawings of a strange-shaped man and an odd, skinny woman bounced all over the screen while loud, exuberant music played in the background.

The old woman, Doña Elena, came again that evening and changed the dressing on Tomás's foot. She said part of the Holy Rosary for him as he lay propped on the couch and I knelt on the floor. Before she left, she placed her hand on mine. It was soft and strong, and I could feel the lines, like gullies in her skin. After she had gone, the imprint of her hand stayed with me. My hand tingled and smelled of her, and I thought of the moss on high rocks near our home and a spring that seeped out of the stones and trickled down the hill.

CHAPTER THREE

We put on our new coats as we got ready to leave Marta's apartment the next afternoon. My coat was the color of wine, and its heaviness reassured me. We fastened Oscar's jacket, and Julia slipped her arms into the sleeves of her black-and-white checkered coat. But when she tried to button it, she found it wouldn't stretch across her big stomach. "Baby," she giggled, patting her tummy, "what do you think you're doing to your mamá's body?"

Marta laughed her hearty laugh, her chest and stomach jiggling, and said, "Like with my seven. Felt like I was busting out all over."

Marta and Julia carried food and I led Oscar. People who passed us in the street were covered with clothes, but I could see their faces. Some were white, some were brown like ours, and some were much darker. Blacks, Marta called them. Everyone rushed through the cold, and I wondered if they always moved so quickly. A woman shouted to three children in English, and two men came toward us carrying a loud radio, which was playing a song in Spanish. I glanced away, but I had seen them watch Julia's face, and I felt sharp fear again for a moment. A small man and woman passed, talking a language I'd never heard.

I stared at the signs on the stores and at the buses that roared down the street. Julia couldn't read. When she was my age, there wasn't a school, but the teacher'd come to our village in time for me. That's why Papá thought I was smart—because I learned to read, and also because I could draw the saints. People praised my pictures. One time Papá said, "María, you've got brains. If anybody can save this family, it's going to be you."

We shivered and stamped our feet. A sign on a bright yellow store announced in Spanish, CHECKS CASHED, MONEY ORDERS, FOOD STAMPS. A man was taping up a sign saying CHICKEN WINGS in a food store. Everywhere I saw big cars and heard radios. Televisions, jewelry, and pretty clothes were for sale in store windows. A long black car pulled up to the curb in front of us, and a man in a white suit got out, followed by five young Latina women. Each woman wore a long formal dress of a different color, and they were laughing, maybe going to a party. They lifted their skirts carefully above the dirt of the sidewalk as they hurried into a building. I could see high-heeled shoes of pink, yellow, blue, violet, and green that matched the colors of the dresses.

Julia pointed to a billboard in Spanish above a grocery store. "María, read that for me," she asked. "The woman looks so happy!"

The sign showed a glowing closeup of a young Latina woman. In one arm, she held a laughing child. With the hand of the other arm, she held up a ticket. We stopped walking and looked up. "EXPERIENCE THE THRILL," I read out loud. "WIN A MILLION DOLLARS. THE ILLINOIS LOTTERY."

"A million dollars?" I asked Marta. "American money? We couldn't win it, could we?"

Marta laughed, shrugged her shoulders, and lifted her hands. "Well, you might, if you bought a ticket. I saw a poor black woman on television once. Something like eight kids, she had. She'd just won. Was having a fit!"

"But not other people here like us?"

"I know some who try. Tomás gave me a ticket for my birthday last year. I planned all night what I'd do with my winnings."

Julia's eyes were bright and shining. We're here in the North, I thought. Where anything's possible.

We walked a little farther, then heard a rumbling and a crashing screech. A train streaked past above us up on a bridge built high over the street. The bridge vibrated with excitement. Our mouths opened as we watched it; then we all had to run to catch up with Marta. In my astonishment, I barely noticed the snow.

Finally, Marta led us to the door of another apartment building. I stopped and pulled on Julia's arm. "Look, Julia, Guardias." A poster of a soldier was in one window, with the letters ARMY at the bottom.

"No, no, no." Marta shook her head. "That's just an army recruiting poster. Somebody stuck it in the window. No need to worry."

Marta opened the door of the building, and we stepped inside. It was dark and smelled of urine. We heard loud rock music thudding behind a door. A black man came hurrying down the steps and went past us; a door next to us opened, and a heavy blonde woman with few teeth stood in it. I bent down, grabbed Oscar, and pulled him into the shadows. A skinny blond boy stared out from under the woman's arm. Marta started slowly in English, "New ones. Just come," and handed the woman our money. The woman shrugged, and the little boy pulled the door closed so we were alone again in the entrance.

"The people upstairs will help you handle her," Marta

23

said, motioning at the blonde woman's door as she led us up the steps, puffing with the effort. She stopped on the third floor, and Julia and I glanced at each other. Julia was pale; we were both frightened, and Oscar clung to me. Marta knocked on a door, and a man, Latino like us, opened it. I heard a television and smelled beans.

"I've brought new ones. Julia Córdoba, and María and Oscar Acosta. Let us inside," Marta said. She turned to us. "It's safe. Don't be afraid."

There were many men and one woman in the room. Three old couches were placed along the walls facing two televisions—a gigantic one, which wasn't working, and a small black-and-white one, which was. A man on the couch by the window held a harmonica, and when the door was shut and locked again, he began to play a song from home.

Marta introduced us to Alicia, a small woman about the age of Mamá. "Alicia'll help you," Marta said, "and, hopefully, find you jobs." She hugged us all against her soft, plump body. "Don't be afraid of the men," she said in her strong voice. "They're good and usually gone working."

"Gracias," I whispered. *"Muchas gracias."*

"Gracias, Marta, for all you've done," Julia repeated. "We'll miss you."

"Come visit. We'll have a party. Honest to God, sometimes we have some beautiful fun. Even up here in the damn cold weather." She smiled broadly at us, left the apartment, and we were alone with the others.

Alicia sighed, introduced us to her husband, and led us from the main room into a smaller room, where a man sat on a mattress on the floor. Another mattress was propped up against a wall. Light came into the room through a window with yellow curtains. A plant with pointed red leaves, growing in a coffee can, and two

24

plastic pink roses were lined up on the windowsill, glowing in the afternoon light. The man nodded and stood up. I noticed that he had a woman's name tattooed on one arm. A line had been tattooed through the name, as if he'd changed his mind. *"Bienvenidos,"* he said, nodded again, and left the room. As he shut the door behind him, I saw two posters of rock singers taped to the door. A carefully hand-drawn sign saying HECTOR AND ROSA FOREVER hung on the opposite wall, and a magazine photo of a smiling child wearing clown makeup had been tacked next to the sign.

Alicia said, "We'll make this your mattress and place," and pulled the small mattress down and onto the floor. She pushed it into position beneath the window, and with the help of her husband, she pinned curtains from a rope that was fastened to the ceiling and divided the room like a clothesline. "Now you'll have privacy," she said.

She led us back through the main room to the room in which they cooked. She explained that the old stove no longer worked, but they had a refrigerator. A hot plate with a pot of soup was on the counter. The faucet wouldn't turn on; they got water from the bathroom tub. But everything was clean, pictures from magazines and calendars were tacked to the walls, and a bucket of lard sat on a table next to another plant in a coffee can.

The sunlight coming through the windows was growing dim. Alicia switched on lights, then gave us corn tortillas and a bowl of soup to share. I looked out the kitchen window, was amazed at how high we were, and saw that there were other buildings even higher. Lights blinked on from building to building, and I wondered how many people were hiding. I stood in the arched doorway to the kitchen, eating my tortillas and watching the men in the main room playing cards. The floor of the main room

25

sloped away from the window, and the deep blue walls had large shapes like clouds where the paint had chipped off. A new tire was placed carefully next to the black-and-white television. I thought, Could someone like us have a car? A clock, shaped like a fan used by a Mexican dancer, ticked on one wall. The face of the clock, centered in the golden fan, was painted blue like the sky and surrounded by a garden of flowers. A butterfly fastened to the second hand of the clock circled through the flowers, like among the lilies at home.

I picked Oscar up and carried him to the clock so he could get a better look. He reached out his hand to touch the butterfly. I stepped back, and the man with the tattoo said to us, "It's Alicia's. She's the one who keeps this place going."

Alicia didn't look at us directly, and she said little as we placed our leftover food in the refrigerator and our clothes in the closet. We thanked her for her help, told the men good night, washed our scrapes and cuts again, and went in to our mattress.

Finally, we had our place. Oscar was soon asleep on our mattress, and Julia sat next to him, her eyes closed, her hands on her pregnant stomach. I squatted next to her on the floor, my back against the wall, and listened to the gentle harmonica.

My eyes grew heavy and I nearly fell asleep, but suddenly, a siren from the street below split the air. I jolted up, my heart pounding, and thought, The Guardias. They've come! Julia also jerked up, and Oscar began to cry. I reached to the mattress and pulled him toward me. He threw his arms around my neck, and I felt the press of his wet face. "María," he sobbed, "the shadow man is coming!" Then we heard the siren move past us and away. Julia breathed deeply, and I rocked Oscar back and forth in my arms.

26

The light in our room flicked on, and Alicia pulled back the curtain. "I heard him cry," she said, gazing at Oscar. "The police go by here often. We've learned not to be afraid." She crossed herself. "I brought you a calendar of Our Lady. I thought she might give you peace. There's a nail for it already on the wall."

She hung the calendar where we'd see it. It showed the crown, face, shoulders, and hands of a statue of the Virgin from a Mexican church. The Virgin was a little different from our Virgin at home, but she looked at us with tender care, and tears rolled down her sad, gentle face. Her arms reached upward, as in comfort, and her white-and-blue veils, gold crown, and embroidered dress reflected her beauty. Alfredo's Mexican Restaurant the calendar said.

"Gracias," we said to Alicia with awe.

"Leave the light on tonight and other nights, if you need to," Alicia said. "It'll help so you're not so afraid." I looked up at the light bulb with relief. Darkness reminded me of the crate.

"You're kind, Alicia," Julia said, her voice tired.

Alicia nodded and stepped back behind the curtain.

I shifted Oscar, who was still whimpering, and looked at the calendar. "See, Oscar Sparrow," I said. "Our Lady is here to keep us safe, almost like in the church at home." He turned toward the calendar and stopped crying.

I smiled. "Good, Oscar. Already she's making you better. Lie back down. You can still see it."

He settled back down onto the mattress but looked up at me. "Story, María. Tell me a story, like Mamá," he begged. I took a deep breath. I didn't know if I could do it after all we'd been through.

"If you can," Julia pleaded with me, her voice exhausted, "maybe it'll calm him."

27

I nodded and swallowed, thinking about the stories Papá'd told us and that Mamá'd continued after we lost Papá. I leaned back against the wall. "In a warm village with a thousand colors," I began, "there lived a little sparrow who loved a little boy." Oscar lay on his side, his cheek on his hands and his eyes staring at the Virgin.

"The sparrow came to the little boy when the sun woke up in the morning, and it left the boy each evening as the sun folded its clothes and lay down for the night." Both Oscar's and Julia's eyes closed.

"Now this was a very brave little sparrow, blessed by the Virgin. It wasn't afraid, not of cruel men or soldiers. The little boy's family lived in a home made of sticks, among butterflies and flowers. But bad men came one time, right when the sun was setting and after the sparrow'd returned to the sky. Only the stars saw what happened." I swallowed and was silent for a few seconds before I continued.

"The men stomped on the flowers. They poisoned the butterflies, and they burned the family's house. In the light of the fire, the children saw the colors of their village melt, then turn gray." Oscar was nearly sleeping, but Julia's dark eyes were now open, and she was listening to the story. I stretched out my legs and kept speaking.

"The next morning, when the sparrow came back with the sun, it found the family crying. The sparrow whispered to the father, 'Come with me. I'll lead you, and I'll take care of your children.'

"And so the family began their journey. They traveled up mountains, into the mist, and they traveled down valleys, down where rivers sang them songs, and ferns and grasses gave them beds to sleep in. Each night they stopped traveling, and each night they waited for the sparrow to return with the sun to guide them the next morning.

28

"Finally, just before dark, they came to a huge river. Soldiers were camped on both sides. The family crouched in the grass, waiting for the morning and the sparrow. But partway through the night, soldiers with guns came after them, and the soldiers grabbed the mamá and papá and led them away. The children lay alone in the dark grass, and even the stars were crying." I stopped and looked at Oscar and Julia. They were both sleeping, but I continued for myself.

"Then the sparrow came down from the night sky. It brought light and rainbows of colors and landed on the little boy's shoulder. 'Don't be afraid,' the sparrow said to the children. 'I'll never leave you now, not even to join the sun. We'll cross the river together. I'll keep you safe; when you are tired I'll stretch until you can rest on my wings, and whenever you need me, I'll give you blessings and colors.' " I closed my eyes, lay down on the mattress, and breathed deeply.

I don't think I dreamed, but I believe I remembered. I was very young and lay on my mat on the floor at home, watching Mamá. The glowing coals of the cooking fire outlined the kind lines on her face and her strong hands as she knelt, fingering her beads, and prayed the Holy Rosary in front of our picture of Our Lady. "Hail, Mary, full of grace. The Lord is with thee," she said. The light of the candle in front of her seemed to enter her eyes and their tiredness ended.

I wanted her, reached out my young child's hands, and whispered, "Mamá."

She turned toward me. "Oh, María. You're awake." I stumbled to her and she picked me up and held me against her. I smelled her smell, the mother smell, of beans, coffee, and cooking fires, and she said, "*Mijita,* I'll take you outside. Our Lady is especially strong tonight."

She carried me out our door, set me on the ground,

and knelt beside me, pointing to the stars. I heard crickets and night birds and smelled coffee blossoms and the breeze. There was no moon and the stars shimmered. "See," Mamá said, "see that band of stars." I looked and the stars swept together. "That's the veil of Our Lady," she said. Then she pointed to other, brighter stars. "And those stars are her crown. She's always with us, just like the stars." She pulled me against her. "What I believe, María, is that when one of our babies dies, the baby becomes a star and joins Our Lady."

"Like Felipe and Celia?" I asked.

"Yes, María. There's Felipe, there's Celia, there's Luís and Paco, and there's the one with no name." She pointed to different parts of the sky and named my dead brothers and sister. "They're all there," she said. She carried me back inside and patted my face. I felt warm and protected, so I closed my eyes. I wondered which star was Papá.

Chapter Four

It was dark when I woke, but I heard sounds and smelled coffee. My body was still stiff and aching from the trip. Julia pulled back our curtain and motioned for me to come with her. We left Oscar sleeping and went through the main room, where men still slept on the couches and the floor, and stepped into the kitchen. Alicia was bent over the hot plate, flipping tortillas on one burner; a pot of coffee boiled on the other. I took deep breaths of the warm, familiar breakfast smells.

Alicia did not look up as Julia spoke to me quietly. "Alicia thinks I shouldn't go with you today. I was sick again during the night. I could stay with Oscar. She'll take you with her and try to get work for the day. I told her you used to use our neighbor's sewing machine." Julia pointed to the kitchen window. "Look, it's snowing."

I turned to the window in wonder. Big flakes of snow were floating down from the sky. A few lights glowed dimly down below, and the streetlamps cast blue circles. Cars and trucks moved slowly on the streets, but the sounds they made were muffled. Julia joined me at the

31

window, and we gazed out at the snow together. Then I focused on the glass of the window. "Look, Julia," I said. The ice on the window had formed shapes like leaves and ferns. "How beautiful," I said. "How did the ice know what'd make us happy?"

Julia also touched the patterns. "It's like the lace shawls women wear to church," she whispered.

Alicia handed me a cup of coffee. "You must eat quickly. We have a long way to travel," she said. "I'll try to get you work with me, but we've got to leave soon to catch the El. I doubt if they'll even notice your age." She crossed herself and went to put on her coat.

Julia handed me a warm tortilla, held out my coat, and tied a scarf under my chin. "I'm sorry you have to do this, Little Sister. Tonight we'll write Mamá." She pressed her hot cheek against mine, hesitated, then turned back to flip tortillas for the men.

I hurried down the dark stairs behind Alicia, who said, "There's enough money to pay your way on the El for a few days." The cold air surprised me as we stepped out the door, and I blinked and felt damp snowflakes brush my eyelids and touch my cheeks.

When Alicia paused to cross the street, I glanced down at the sleeve of my coat. Snowflakes, fragile bits of ice, lay against the wine-colored cloth. I touched one, amazed by its beauty, and it melted into my finger. I bent down, scooped up a little snow with my hands, and put it in my mouth. I was startled by the coldness and tasted grit mixed in with the snow. Alicia grabbed my arm and hurried me along.

We stopped at a platform beneath a little roof, and Alicia stood quietly, her eyes nearly closed, her chin tucked into her scarf, and her bare hands stuck into her coat sleeves. Empty train tracks led away from us, merging at a distance, and wire hung from one soot-covered building to another. Everything seemed gray.

I thought about the pink, yellow, and blue buildings in the village at home, remembered the hot, burning sun, and pictured the sparrow from my story. In my mind, it perched on my shoulder and lit up all the gray buildings with color. Then I shivered. Although the snow had stopped falling, a cold wind was blowing against my coat and cotton skirt, and my long hair whipped across my face from under my scarf.

Suddenly, the ground shook, and I heard the screech again, rushing at me, crashing into my head. I slammed shut my eyes, threw up my arms to protect my face, and felt Alicia pull me. "Come! Now! It's the El. Step inside!" she ordered. I stumbled forward with her and looked around. We had stepped into a train car and were pressed tightly against other people. A door banged shut behind us, and we were jerked into motion, faster than I had ever traveled before. I grabbed for a metal bar and stood swaying with the movement, then glanced at a young blonde woman standing next to me. Her eyes were outlined with bright blue, and she smiled at me with a painted red mouth. I smiled back before looking down and wondered what she thought of my darkness.

The El stopped and started many times and I watched Alicia. Her limp hair hung down her back from under her scarf, and her face, like Mamá's, seemed swollen with age and sadness. The lines of her eyebrows, also like Mamá's, almost touched the circles under her eyes. She wore wet tennis shoes without socks, and her legs were pale and streaked with light blue veins. Finally, she motioned to me with her head. "The next time, we get off."

She led me off the El and down several blocks bordered with crumbling buildings and their broken windows. One lot was empty, with only charred boards and trash. I thought of the garbage dump at home where the Guardias left dead bodies. Then Alicia said, "In here." She crossed herself again. "Try not to act like you're afraid."

I followed her into a dark doorway and up some stairs. A man with white hair stood in a partially opened door at the top and snapped in Spanish, "You're late. That one, how old is she?"

Alicia started to say, "My daughter," but he reached for me, grabbed me by my coat, and pulled me toward him.

I remembered the man who had nailed us into the crate and squeezed my hand into a fist. "Eighteen," I answered.

He held me so close, I could smell his breath. "I'll check her card later," he said and shoved me into a room.

The room was crowded with women, sewing machines, and clothes piled high on platforms. Each woman sat at a little table, her hands moving the material furiously under the machine, and the room buzzed with the sound of sewing. Alicia hurried into an empty place, motioned me to sit at the table next to her, and quietly showed me how to work the machine. The man came over to us and stood in front of me. Alicia glanced up at him, then returned her eyes to the table. She picked up a stack of cloth and said, "Watch me."

"Gracias," I whispered.

Within a short time I could sew the seam straight, but I felt sweat on my forehead as the man with the white hair paced back and forth. My hands cramped and my neck ached. When the man was on the other side of the room, I looked at the other women. Most were Latinas, like Alicia and me, but some had slanted eyes. They all stared down at their work.

Time passed, and I worked without stopping at the machines and began to wonder if I had a fever. My cheeks burned, and my mind wandered until I thought I heard muffled voices from a crate. Suddenly, a drop of cold water plopped onto my face. I blinked and went on with my work. Then another drop hit my cheek. I bent my head backward and looked up at the high ceiling. Bare bulbs hung from wires, the plaster was cracked and leaking, and water stains made circles above my head. Drops of water seeped into one of the cracks above me, then, one by one, dripped down onto my hot face. *"Gracias,"* I said to Our Lady.

The man stopped our work partway through the day. "Break." He scowled, his eyebrows tight, as he walked out the door. I turned around nervously. Alicia shrugged her shoulders. "Time to eat," she said, then handed me some food she had brought. Alicia smiled a little and joined a group of women already chatting and laughing.

I ate the cold beans and tortillas in quick bites, satisfying my hunger, and watched a happy-looking group of women talking rapidly in a language I had never heard before. I heard a movement next to me. A Latina girl, not much older than me, pulled her chair next to mine. She smiled and said, "You new here?" I nodded.

"I came a month ago. Sure is different here. *Ave María Purísima,* is it cold! Not fit weather for Christians." She laughed. The girl began to peel an orange. "But there's more food than at home."

I watched her pull the thick skin from the fruit. The juice ran like light onto her fingers. I thought of Julia's gold chain.

"Want half?" she asked, raising her eyebrows. I shook my head politely.

"Yes, take it." She smiled and handed it to me.

I lowered my eyes. *"Gracias,"* I said as I pulled off a

35

slice and bit into it. The sweetness and moisture were as refreshing as the spring water you'd find after walking half a day in the mountains. As I smiled at her, she shook her hair and took off her dark sweater. The blouse she wore underneath was bright pink and yellow. "My name is Isabel," she said, as she tied a yellow ribbon around her hair. Then the man came back into the room, and she made a face. I giggled as I returned to work but saw no more of Isabel that day.

The El throbbed as it hurried Alicia and me home that night, and cold air leaked in through the windows and up from the floor. I swayed with exhaustion in my seat. Alicia watched me for some time; then she whispered, "Lean against me, María. That will make you warmer."

Her face seemed kind, so I rested against her, my eyes half closed, staring out the window. Distant lights glowed, like fireflies from home, and I heard the night birds from our village. Isabel had reminded me of a lost friend from school, Alicia reminded me of Mamá, and the longing rose so high that I trembled. Alicia opened her arm toward me and pressed me against her.

"You've lost so much," she whispered, "and I have too. I lost a daughter and a son, about your age. If I've seemed unfriendly, that's why. It hurts to look at you."

I turned and stared at Alicia, hearing the screaming and smelling the blood. Alicia crossed herself and wiped the back of her hand across her eyes.

"Like Papá and Ramón," I said. "I'm sorry, Alicia."

She sat quietly, her eyes down, until the two women near us got off the El. After they left, she turned to me and said, "You can tell me, if you want to. About what happened and about your mother and baby sister."

"I don't know if I can. Julia and Mamá talked to friends in Mexico, but I've never told anyone," I whispered.

"I understand." Her eyes were gentle. "Don't talk unless you want to."

I sat silently a little longer. Finally, I began. "I can't remember much of it. It happened at night. The Guardias broke in our house and killed Papá and Ramón, Julia's husband. But the next morning I can remember. Papá and Ramón were dead, and Julia was gone." My hands shook. "We found her in the ravine, past the dump with the other bodies. They had hurt her in bad ways, but she was alive."

I looked at Alicia through tears. "I wake up at night sometimes, screaming, because I almost remember." I stopped talking for a moment. Alicia nodded with tears in her eyes.

"After we found Julia, Mamá said we had to leave. If we didn't, they'd kill us all, even Oscar and Teresa, because Papá had worked with the teacher to get our school." My voice dropped. "It was so bad, we had to step over bodies."

Alicia nodded. "I know. May God save your souls."

"So we walked up through the mountains, north into Guatemala. But it was dangerous there too because the soldiers were killing the Indians." I sat quietly, then said, "The Indians wore such beautiful clothes, like all the colors in the rainbow."

"I know," Alicia said.

"Lots of the time we didn't eat, but sometimes people gave us food. A couple of times, we got work. But Alicia"—my voice cracked—"Julia was sick and thought she might be pregnant. Then her stomach started to swell. She'd cry and cry and hold her hands against her stomach. 'Ramón's, Ramón's,' she'd say, 'don't let it be the Guardias'.' Mamá and I, we almost couldn't stand it. It hurt so bad." Alicia hugged me.

"We walked for months in Mexico before we got a ride

37

to Monterrey," I continued. "Julia got a job in a textile factory for awhile, and I cleaned for rich people, and we moved into a little shack, near some other Salvadorans. But we still didn't have enough to eat. Teresa, my baby sister, was sick with worms and a fever, but Oscar was okay, just thin." Alicia shook her head, back and forth.

"But some of the Mexican police found our friends, and when our friends couldn't bribe them, the Mexicans sent them back to El Salvador." I looked at my hands. "They'll kill us if we go home. And the war's still going on."

The El stopped at a station, and people got on at the other end. We sat in silence and I remembered Papá, the last time before the Guardias came. I had knelt in the dirt behind the house, tracing words for him with a stick. The sun was red like a wound in the early evening sky. Papá sat on the ground, leaning his back against the wall, and said, "You can read and write. And you've got the gift of an artist. They can't take that away."

Papá had closed his eyes and tipped his face up into the wind. "Come and sit with me," he said, not opening his eyes. I moved over next to him. "You're the one who'll save the family," he whispered. I said nothing but smelled on him the sugar cane fields where he'd worked that day. The church bells called out the coming night, and the *chachalacas* sang out in the dark.

"I keep thinking about Papá saying I was going to save the family, Alicia," I said. "I don't know if I can do it." I cried, leaning against Alicia, my eyes so full of tears I couldn't see the lights.

Alicia stroked my forehead. "Sometimes it helps to talk, María," she said. "Do you want to tell me more?"

I nodded. "I don't like to tell Julia how bad I feel; she already hurts so much. But sometimes I think I'm going to break inside."

"I know," Alicia said and crossed me on my forehead.

"One of the Mexican women in Monterrey helped us. She's the one who'll read the letters we write to Mamá. She knew about people going north, in crates." I choked on the last words. "We had enough money to pay for three of us. That would leave a little medicine for Teresa. Mamá said we should go. Teresa was too sick to make it. Mamá said, 'Take Oscar and go. It's our only chance. Your father would want it.' When Teresa's better and we've got money for a *coyote*, they'll come north and join us. So we left. Mamá came with us as far as the river and cried when we said good-bye."

Alicia held me against her, but I pulled back, urgent to tell her everything. "We waited by the river before we got on the rafts. I could hear the frogs and see the shadows of the other people. The stars were clear, Alicia, like the Virgin's veil. The last thing Mamá said to me was 'Take care of Oscar, and try to help Julia with the baby. You're the one who can read and write. Papá believed in you.' "

I put my face in my hands, and tears ran through my fingers. "We had to pull Oscar away from Mamá," I said.

Alicia and I sat in silence, the El rocking as we traveled. Finally, I said quietly, "Alicia, back home, I heard the villagers whisper that the *norteamericanos*, the people up here, had helped our leaders hurt us, that the guns they used came from the United States. Do you believe that?"

"I heard it too. I don't know, María. I don't know. Everything's so hard to believe. So terrible."

When we arrived home, Oscar was already asleep, and Julia had a few pieces of paper and a pencil. We wrote Mamá to tell her we were alive and that I had work. Then I drew a lily on the edge of the letter. I fell asleep holding the pencil and dreamed I was home, under the *amate* tree, drawing flowers while Alicia visited with Mamá. As they talked in my dream, a dove cooed in the distance.

The pain in my chest was a little better after talking to Alicia, and she and I worked for days, traveling on the El to and from the shop. I often talked briefly with Isabel at lunch, while the other women laughed and chatted. One day I took Isabel a drawing I'd done of birds and flowers from home, and her eyes glowed when she saw it.

That same night we received Mamá's first letter. Her friend Beatriz had written it down for her, but they were Mamá's words. "My children," she said, "I can't tell you how grateful I am that you are safe. God has answered my prayers. I think of you all the time and look at your baby sister and see each of you. Teresa has your color, Julia, and your face, María, and she stands and moves like you, Oscar, my son. You are all very brave, and Papá would be so proud of you. Have strength, my children. I know there is hope for us all. Mamá." At the bottom of the page, Mamá had drawn a little face for Oscar, and the paper felt warm in my hand as I handed it to him.

Julia looked into my eyes. "Thank goodness you learned to read and write," she said.

Julia found work a few days later, washing dishes. Oscar stayed in the apartment alone as we worked, and watched television. At times he stared out the window or played with little stones I had found him. At night, when I'd come home, I'd hold him up so he could watch the clock with the butterfly circling through the flowers. I also told him stories and Julia sang him songs. The man with the crossed-off tattoo slept in the same room we did but didn't bother us. I'd often sit with my back against the wall as Oscar fell asleep. Sometimes I'd wonder about the little sign that said HECTOR AND ROSA FOREVER. Who were they? I thought. What happened to them? Would I ever feel like that? I'd look at the posters of the rock singers and try to imagine what it'd be like at a concert. Then I'd say a little prayer to the calendar with the Virgin.

Finally, I was paid, and we wrote Mamá again and arranged with Alicia to send Mamá money. That night a man with a guitar came to play music with the harmonica man. The other men began to sing along with them in the main room, and Julia, Oscar, and I stood in the doorway listening. It was happy music, from home, and Julia began to sing with them. One by one, the men stopped singing and turned to her, listening to her voice. Julia closed her eyes, wrapped her arms together, and swayed with the rhythm, smiling as she sang. The men clapped when the song was over, and Julia opened her eyes, blushing.

"More, sing more," the guitar player said, the other men agreeing. Julia glanced down once, shyly, looked up, and first began humming, then singing with her clear voice, the stanzas of a song Papá had taught us after his travels when he looked for work.

> "Lovely are those mountains,
> Skyward they are soaring.
> Let the sheep be gathered
> For daylight is dawning."

Again, we clapped, then sang other happy songs together, the strong chords from the guitar breaking through the grayness of Chicago until I felt like dancing. Even Oscar was in good spirits. I fell asleep that night feeling happy and proud of the money I had earned for all of us. I knew I had Papá's blessing.

41

CHAPTER FIVE

Alicia and I worked from dark to dark and hardly saw the light. Several times we heard sirens. Alicia always crossed herself when that happened, and I saw the other women pause in their work. I knew that they also must have come here secretly and were frightened too.

One morning, I looked over at Isabel while she worked and saw tears running down her face. When we stopped for lunch, I went to her and asked her what had happened. "My aunt," she cried. "Immigration. She got real sick, and when she went to the hospital, someone turned her in." I gave Isabel a hug and shivered with fear. Isabel didn't cry again, but after that day she looked older.

Often while I worked at the sewing machine, the man with the white hair stood behind me with his hands on my shoulders. My face burned during those times, and my shoulders ached from his hand print. Alicia glanced over at me and told him I was her daughter, but he continued. Sometimes tears of shame rolled down my face. Why is he doing this to me? I thought. I'm dark. Others are lighter. I wondered if it was the way I moved or sat, and my shame deepened.

After work, I saw other women look at me with sympathy, and Isabel squeezed my hand. I noticed that she no longer dressed in bright colors but just wore one outfit of gray and brown. One night, as Alicia and I walked to the El, Alicia said, "I don't think it will be safe for you at work much longer. I think he's really going to hurt you."

"Do you think if I learned more English, I could get a different job?" I asked with fear in my heart.

"Maybe, God willing."

"Who could teach me?"

"I don't know. Let me think." She held my arm as we hurried down the dark street.

The next day was Sunday, and Alicia and I didn't need to work. I awoke to the smell of coffee. Julia had already gone to the restaurant for the day, Alicia sat in a chair near the hot plate, and Oscar stood at the window, his weight on his right foot and the ball of his left, as he stared outside. He glanced at me, and I went to him and blinked at the sun, which was almost as bright as during the dry season at home. "I'll be with you today, Oscar Sparrow, and I'll take you outside so you can get some light. We can see all the things rich people have up here in the North." He glanced into my eyes and smiled.

"There's no food this morning, María," Alicia told me. "Just a little coffee. Also, I've thought some more about the danger for you at work. It's a good idea for you to learn more English. I think you should go to Marta's house and see if anyone there can teach you. But you'll probably have to keep working with me for awhile." I thought of the man with the white hair and trembled with fear and shame. Alicia came over to me and put her arm around my shoulder. "Take Oscar and go out into the

43

sun, María," she said. "You're young; you need plea-sure. I think there will be food by evening."

"*Gracias,*" I said. "You've helped me so much, like Mamá."

Ignoring my hunger, I dressed Oscar in winter clothes and took him down the steps, past the other apartments, to the outside door. The little blond boy watched us from the manager's apartment, and we hurried outside. The sun was bright and glared on the snow.

I held Oscar's hand tightly, and we walked down the street, forgetting our troubles and watching people, build-ings, and cars. I read the signs that were in Spanish. GOT A PROBLEM? TRY JESUS. HE LOVES YOU said a bench at a bus stop. UNITED PEOPLES' PARTY announced a banner hanging from a window. THANKS FOR KEEPING THE NEIGH-BORHOOD CLEAN! said a large piece of wood, carefully nailed onto a boarded-up building. VOICES OF PUERTO RICO SPOKEN HERE declared several stores. Signs in English appeared everywhere, and people wore good clothes and carried many packages. I wondered if children weren't out begging just because it was too cold.

Many cars were parked by a bright building with a sign showing a big yellow *M*. We stepped inside. People were clustered at a red counter while girls rushed behind it, handing people food in white paper bags. My stomach twisted at the smell of food. I watched a girl about my age and color carry her baby and bag of food to a table. The baby wore a bright blue suit, the color of our sky, and banged the table with his fat hands as she un-wrapped the food. I wondered how much Teresa had grown since we saw her.

Suddenly, I saw a policeman eating in a corner. My heart pounded in my ears, and I grabbed Oscar's hand and dragged him across the street, not even watching for cars. Then I ran down the block and around the corner,

44

hard in all directions, her lips sputtering. The candles flickered, then burned once more.

"Again," Tomás said, and Verónica blew all over the table. ·

"Once more!" Tomás cried, and as the little girl blew again, he blew. The flames went out, and everyone laughed and clapped. Verónica's face glowed. Oscar's eyes were shining, and his smiling mouth was open.

Marta's younger daughter was on the table and about to plop one hand in the middle of the cake, when Marta swooped her up and sat her firmly on a chair. "Here," she said, quickly cutting a chunk of cake and handing it to the toddler. The little girl ate with both hands, covering her face with frosting. I smiled, thinking of my baby sister Teresa, and Marta stood back, her hands on her broad hips as she watched her daughters. "Well, I was never the quiet, sedate type when I was young, either." She winked at Tomás and laughed. "Doesn't run in the family, does it, Tomás?"

"What can I say?" he said, laughing. I looked at him quickly. He looked directly at me and smiled, arched his eyebrows high, shrugged his shoulders, and gestured upward with his hands.

"You'll have some cake with us, María," Marta said to me. "But first, here's a piece for the birthday girl, then you, Oscar." She gave Oscar cake on a paper napkin, and he ate it greedily.

"Gracias," I said for Oscar.

Marta cut other pieces, smiling at Verónica, who was maneuvering a big fork. "My sister, Tomás's mother, wanted him to be a priest," Marta chatted to me. "She sent him off to seminary when he was eleven. But he ran away." She looked at Tomás fondly. "He lived on the beach for awhile. Came home so scraggly we hardly recognized him."

48

pulling Oscar behind me. Finally, I stopped. Bent over and gasping for air, I realized how hard Oscar was crying. "Shadow man, shadow man," he sobbed, reaching for me, but I pulled away from him and looked around the corner.

I saw no police and gradually calmed down. As Oscar's cries turned to whimpers, I wiped his wet face with my scarf. "We're okay, Oscar," I said, smiling. "The police didn't follow us. Let's walk around some more before we go to Marta's."

We moved slowly, staring in store windows, then came to a child-sized orange-and-red plastic horse outside a toy store. Oscar ran up to it and grabbed the saddle. I looked around nervously, but no one seemed to be paying attention to us so I pushed him up onto the horse. "Yeah," he cried, slapping the horse's neck and bouncing up and down as I stood smiling at him. Finally, I said, "Oscar, let's go inside."

It was warm, and music was playing. Huge plastic sea animals, fish with teeth and brown and green turtles, were blown up like balloons and hung from the ceiling. Shelves of dolls and stuffed animals went down one aisle, and another whole aisle was filled with toy weapons. I shuddered when I saw a toy machine gun.

"Look," Oscar said, as he went up to a large plastic monster. It had a green snake's head, huge muscles in a humanlike body, hands that looked like they wanted to grab you, and clawed, lizardlike feet. "Ugh," I said. "I don't like it."

A clown with a red painted smile came out of a back room and began to blow up balloons for children. A woman bought a pale purple balloon for a small girl and tied it around her hand. Oscar's eyes sparkled as he stared up at the balloon, and his mouth was open. I remembered how he used to march around our house,

45

barefooted in the dust, our dirt-brown dog following behind him, his eyes glowing as he blew his new clay whistle. I bent down to look directly in his eyes. "Oscar," I said, "someday I'll get you a balloon. I promise." He beamed.

As we were leaving, I saw a package of big pens in all the colors of the rainbow. I stared at them; then Oscar tugged at me, and I realized a woman was standing near us. I grabbed Oscar and stepped backward, but the woman smiled, saying something to me in English as she reached for one of the pens and, in a single stroke, drew a wide ribbon of deep pink across a cardboard sign. I gazed at the color. Then the woman said more words to me in English. I jerked my eyes from the color and, with Oscar against me, backed away. "Gracias," I said, "gracias," and pulled Oscar out the door.

EL PALACIO DE LA MODA FEMENINA the sign on the next store read, and the window was filled with beautiful bride dresses, all in white with ruffles and laces. I walked in front of the window, looking in. I didn't know people could be so rich. On Julia's wedding day, she wore a white dress, with flowers in her hair. There was music from the violin, guitar, and marimba at the wedding dance, and we could smell pink coffee blossoms and *el gallo en chicha*, chicken, cooking.

"We must go to Marta's now," I said to Oscar. My body felt carved out by hunger again, as it always did when there was no food in the morning. I wished for *pepescas*, small fried fish we ate at home.

Smelling chili, I heard men's voices when I knocked on Marta's door. A strange man opened the door a little, and I looked down, away from his eyes. "I've come to speak to Marta, please," I explained. He opened the door the rest of the way, and we stepped inside. I saw the colors of Marta's bright main room, the room where we'd stayed when we'd first arrived—the cross of plastic flowers, the poster of the red-haired woman, San Antonio on the television. Marta's girls laughed in another room, and Tomás limped across the room toward me. When he saw us, he smiled.

"Marta?" I said, not meeting his eyes.

"In the kitchen," he answered, his voice soft and clear. "Verónica's three today. We're having a birthday party."

"Oh," I responded and stood, not moving.

"Come on," he said. "I'm glad you're here."

Marta was in the kitchen, trying to light a match at the same time she kept her younger daughter from climbing on the table. Her older daughter, sitting on a chair, licked frosting from her fingers and stared at a little white cake with three tiny pink candles.

"María. Oscar," Marta said happily, her brown eyes warm and smiling. "What a good time for you to join us."

"We're having a full-fledged American party," said Tomás. "Complete with candles." I glanced at him. He was watching me with his blue eyes. Oscar grabbed the table and stared at the cake. We were so hungry.

"Try to sing with us, in English," Marta said, as she lifted her squirming younger daughter into her left arm and managed to light the candles.

The candles glowed, two men joined us in the kitchen, and they all sang in English. I smiled and recognized the tune. The three-year-old's face beamed as they sang "Ver-ón-i-ca," spreading out her name.

"Now blow hard," Marta said in Spanish, when the song was over. Verónica stood up in her chair and stretched out over the table with her dimpled hands planted on each side of the cake. The glow of the candles lit her round face, and she took a deep breath and blew

46   47

"But with money, Marta. Money." Tomás laughed.

"Yep, he's some big-time genius when it comes to getting jobs," Marta said proudly. Then she watched Oscar eat. "Oscar looks hungry," she said to me. "Have either of you eaten?"

I gulped. "Yes, I have. But Oscar hasn't."

"Tomás," Marta said, "when you are done eating, give the boy some bread and heat him some milk."

"Here, María." She smiled at me and handed me some cake. "I'll pour us some coffee." I tried not to eat too quickly, but the sweetness of the food filled my mouth and warmed me to my chest. The two men took their cake and left the room.

"The boy looks better," Marta said to me, going to the stove.

"Yes. Pretty much. He's still quiet."

"And do you have work?" Marta asked me. "And does Julia?"

I nodded, thinking of the man with the white hair. "Yes, with Alicia. And Julia's washing dishes."

"That is good. God's provided," Marta replied, pouring the coffee and handing me a cup. She took her hanky out of her blouse and wiped her broad forehead as Tomás gave bread and warmed milk to Oscar and the little girls. Then Tomás leaned against the wall with his coffee, as if he was waiting.

My free hand hung at my side, and I felt awkward. I hadn't expected to talk in front of Tomás. The little girls finished their food and climbed out of their chairs. Marta handed the younger one a bottle with water, and they ran out of the room in the direction of the television.

I cleared my throat. "Alicia thinks I need to speak English. She doesn't think my work with her'll last much longer." I wondered if Marta and Tomás could tell by looking at me what the man with the white hair was do-

49

ing. "Alicia said that you might know someone to teach me," I said to Marta.

Taking a red scarf out of her pocketbook, Marta tied back her hair. "Tomás is the only one I can think of, he and Doña Elena, the midwife. I don't know much, and I don't think we should ask Doña Elena. She's too busy." She seemed to be thinking, then sat back down. "Alicia's right, you know. Either you or Julia needs to learn. This sure ain't no land of milk and honey. Not for two good-looking girls like you. Especially with no one to protect you."

I felt my entire body turn red. Marta didn't seem to notice. "What do you think, Tomás?" she said, turning toward him. "Could you teach her?"

My face was wet with sweat, and my legs were weak. I hadn't thought of Tomás. I was embarrassed even to see him after being pressed against him in the crate, especially after what Marta had just said.

Tomás didn't look at me, either. I was thankful. "Yes, I could teach her what I know," he said gently.

"Good," Marta responded, slapping her hands down on the table. "Come here, María, whenever you're not working, and if Tomás is home, he can help you. He just works day by day." Her face showed pride. "Tomás is very intelligent, and his hands are always busy. He's the hope of the family."

Marta's daughters clamored back into the kitchen carrying a red ball, and Tomás spent the rest of the day saying phrases to me in English. "I need work," he said slowly, not looking at me directly.

"I need work," I carefully repeated.

He said nothing personal to me as we practiced, but when Oscar and I put on our coats to go back into the cold, he handed us each several slices of bread and a piece of meat. "Take these," he said and looked away. I could only whisper my thanks.

At home we shared our bread and meat with Julia and Alicia, and told them about my English lessons and the party. Oscar puffed his cheeks, blew hard, and clapped to demonstrate. "See, Little Sister," Julia smiled and said, stroking my hair, "there's good luck up here. There is. We just have to be patient." That night Julia made up a song about the sparrow with its rainbow of colors as we fell asleep.

CHAPTER SIX

The next day I again went to work with Alicia. I circled around the man with the white hair as I entered the factory room and didn't look up as I worked. The other women stared down also, and there were no sounds except for the buzzing of the sewing machines and an occasional siren outside. We all worked on the same dark green cloth, and I had to squint to see the seams. I glanced at Isabel once. During the morning and early afternoon, the man with the white hair didn't come near me. Then, through the sides of my eyes, I saw him cross the room and move behind me. "Get up and come with me," he said.

I panicked and looked at Alicia. Her face was white and she started to get up. "Now!" he ordered. I pushed my chair back, my heart pounding, and followed him into a little hall behind the main room, out of sight of the other women. The man laughed and grabbed me by my shoulders, and as I twisted to get away from him, he snarled, "You're illegal. I can do anything." He laughed pulling Oscar behind me. Finally, I stopped. Bent over and gasping for air, I realized how hard Oscar was crying. "Shadow man, shadow man," he sobbed, reaching for me, but I pulled away from him and looked around the corner.

I saw no police and gradually calmed down. As Oscar's cries turned to whimpers, I wiped his wet face with my scarf. "We're okay, Oscar," I said, smiling. "The police didn't follow us. Let's walk around some more before we go to Marta's."

We moved slowly, staring in store windows, then came to a child-sized orange-and-red plastic horse outside a toy store. Oscar ran up to it and grabbed the saddle. I looked around nervously, but no one seemed to be paying attention to us so I pushed him up onto the horse. "Yeah," he cried, slapping the horse's neck and bouncing up and down as I stood smiling at him. Finally, I said, "Oscar, let's go inside."

It was warm, and music was playing. Huge plastic sea animals, fish with teeth and brown and green turtles, were blown up like balloons and hung from the ceiling. Shelves of dolls and stuffed animals went down one aisle, and another whole aisle was filled with toy weapons. I shuddered when I saw a toy machine gun.

"Look," Oscar said, as he went up to a large plastic monster. It had a green snake's head, huge muscles in a humanlike body, hands that looked like they wanted to grab you, and clawed, lizardlike feet. "Ugh," I said. "I don't like it."

A clown with a red painted smile came out of a back room and began to blow up balloons for children. A woman bought a pale purple balloon for a small girl and tied it around her hand. Oscar's eyes sparkled as he stared up at the balloon, and his mouth was open. I remembered how he used to march around our house,

45

barefooted in the dust, our dirt-brown dog following behind him, his eyes glowing as he blew his new clay whistle. I bent down to look directly in his eyes. "Oscar," I said, "someday I'll get you a balloon. I promise." He beamed.

As we were leaving, I saw a package of big pens in all the colors of the rainbow. I stared at them; then Oscar tugged at me, and I realized a woman was standing near us. I grabbed Oscar and stepped backward, but the woman smiled, saying something to me in English as she reached for one of the pens and, in a single stroke, drew a wide ribbon of deep pink across a cardboard sign. I gazed at the color. Then the woman said more words to me in English. I jerked my eyes from the color and, with Oscar against me, backed away. *"Gracias,"* I said, *"gracias,"* and pulled Oscar out the door.

EL PALACIO DE LA MODA FEMENINA the sign on the next store read, and the window was filled with beautiful bride dresses, all in white with ruffles and laces. I walked in front of the window, looking in. I didn't know people could be so rich. On Julia's wedding day, she wore a white dress, with flowers in her hair. There was music from the violin, guitar, and marimba at the wedding dance, and we could smell pink coffee blossoms and *el gallo en chicha,* chicken, cooking.

"We must go to Marta's now," I said to Oscar. My body felt carved out by hunger again, as it always did when there was no food in the morning. I wished for *pepescas,* small fried fish we ate at home.

Smelling chili, I heard men's voices when I knocked on Marta's door. A strange man opened the door a little, and I looked down, away from his eyes. "I've come to speak to Marta, please," I explained. He opened the door the rest of the way, and we stepped inside. I saw the colors of Marta's bright main room, the room where we'd stayed when we'd first arrived—the cross of plastic flowers, the poster of the red-haired woman, San Antonio on the television. Marta's girls laughed in another room, and Tomás limped across the room toward me. When he saw us, he smiled.

"Marta?" I said, not meeting his eyes.

"In the kitchen," he answered, his voice soft and clear. "Verónica's three today. We're having a birthday party."

"Oh," I responded and stood, not moving.

"Come on," he said. "I'm glad you're here."

Marta was in the kitchen, trying to light a match at the same time she kept her younger daughter from climbing on the table. Her older daughter, sitting on a chair, licked frosting from her fingers and stared at a little white cake with three tiny pink candles.

"María. Oscar," Marta said happily, her brown eyes warm and smiling. "What a good time for you to join us."

"We're having a full-fledged American party," said Tomás. "Complete with candles." I glanced at him. He was watching me with his blue eyes. Oscar grabbed the table and stared at the cake. We were so hungry.

"Try to sing with us, in English," Marta said, as she lifted her squirming younger daughter into her left arm and managed to light the candles.

The candles glowed, two men joined us in the kitchen, and they all sang in English. I smiled and recognized the tune. The three-year-old's face beamed as they sang "Ver-ón-i-ca," spreading out her name.

"Now blow hard," Marta said in Spanish, when the song was over. Verónica stood up in her chair and stretched out over the table with her dimpled hands planted on each side of the cake. The glow of the candles lit her round face, and she took a deep breath and blew

47

hard in all directions, her lips sputtering. The candles flickered, then burned once more.

"Again," Tomás said, and Verónica blew all over the table.

"Once more!" Tomás cried, and as the little girl blew again, he blew. The flames went out, and everyone laughed and clapped. Verónica's face glowed. Oscar's eyes were shining, and his smiling mouth was open.

Marta's younger daughter was on the table and about to plop one hand in the middle of the cake, when Marta swooped her up and sat her firmly on a chair. "Here," she said, quickly cutting a chunk of cake and handing it to the toddler. The little girl ate with both hands, covering her face with frosting. I smiled, thinking of my baby sister Teresa, and Marta stood back, her hands on her broad hips as she watched her daughters. "Well, I was never the quiet, sedate type when I was young, either." She winked at Tomás and laughed. "Doesn't run in the family, does it, Tomás?"

"What can I say?" he said, laughing. I looked at him quickly. He looked directly at me and smiled, arched his eyebrows high, shrugged his shoulders, and gestured upward with his hands.

"You'll have some cake with us, María," Marta said to me. "But first, here's a piece for the birthday girl, then you, Oscar." She gave Oscar cake on a paper napkin, and he ate it greedily.

"Gracias," I said for Oscar.

Marta cut other pieces, smiling at Verónica, who was maneuvering a big fork. "My sister, Tomás's mother, wanted him to be a priest," Marta chatted to me. "She sent him off to seminary when he was eleven. But he ran away." She looked at Tomás fondly. "He lived on the beach for awhile. Came home so scraggly we hardly recognized him."

"But with money, Marta. Money." Tomás laughed.

"Yep, he's some big-time genius when it comes to getting jobs," Marta said proudly. Then she watched Oscar eat. "Oscar looks hungry," she said to me. "Have either of you eaten?"

I gulped. "Yes, I have. But Oscar hasn't."

"Tomás," Marta said, "when you are done eating, give the boy some bread and heat him some milk."

"Here, María." She smiled at me and handed me some cake. "I'll pour us some coffee." I tried not to eat too quickly, but the sweetness of the food filled my mouth and warmed me to my chest. The two men took their cake and left the room.

"The boy looks better," Marta said to me, going to the stove.

"Yes. Pretty much. He's still quiet."

"And do you have work?" Marta asked me. "And does Julia?"

I nodded, thinking of the man with the white hair. "Yes, with Alicia. And Julia's washing dishes."

"That is good. God's provided," Marta replied, pouring the coffee and handing me a cup. She took her hanky out of her blouse and wiped her broad forehead as Tomás gave bread and warmed milk to Oscar and the little girls. Then Tomás leaned against the wall with his coffee, as if he was waiting.

My free hand hung at my side, and I felt awkward. I hadn't expected to talk in front of Tomás. The little girls finished their food and climbed out of their chairs. Marta handed the younger one a bottle with water, and they ran out of the room in the direction of the television.

I cleared my throat. "Alicia thinks I need to speak English. She doesn't think my work with her'll last much longer." I wondered if Marta and Tomás could tell by looking at me what the man with the white hair was doing. "Alicia said that you might know someone to teach me," I said to Marta.

Taking a red scarf out of her pocketbook, Marta tied back her hair. "Tomás is the only one I can think of, he and Doña Elena, the midwife. I don't know much, and I don't think we should ask Doña Elena. She's too busy." She seemed to be thinking, then sat back down. "Alicia's right, you know. Either you or Julia needs to learn. This sure ain't no land of milk and honey. Not for two good-looking girls like you. Especially with no one to protect you."

I felt my entire body turn red. Marta didn't seem to notice. "What do you think, Tomás?" she said, turning toward him. "Could you teach her?"

My face was wet with sweat, and my legs were weak. I hadn't thought of Tomás. I was embarrassed even to see him after being pressed against him in the crate, especially after what Marta had just said.

Tomás didn't look at me, either. I was thankful. "Yes, I could teach her what I know," he said gently.

"Good," Marta responded, slapping her hands down on the table. "Come here, María, whenever you're not working, and if Tomás is home, he can help you. He just works day by day." Her face showed pride. "Tomás is very intelligent, and his hands are always busy. He's the hope of the family."

Marta's daughters clamored back into the kitchen carrying a red ball, and Tomás spent the rest of the day saying phrases to me in English. "I need work," he said slowly, not looking at me directly.

"I need work," I carefully repeated.

He said nothing personal to me as we practiced, but when Oscar and I put on our coats to go back into the cold, he handed us each several slices of bread and a piece of meat. "Take these," he said and looked away. I could only whisper my thanks.

At home we shared our bread and meat with Julia and Alicia, and told them about my English lessons and the party. Oscar puffed his cheeks, blew hard, and clapped to demonstrate. "See, Little Sister," Julia smiled and said, stroking my hair, "there's good luck up here. There is. We just have to be patient." That night Julia made up a song about the sparrow with its rainbow of colors as we fell asleep.

CHAPTER SIX

The next day I again went to work with Alicia. I circled around the man with the white hair as I entered the factory room and didn't look up as I worked. The other women stared down also, and there were no sounds except for the buzzing of the sewing machines and an occasional siren outside. We all worked on the same dark green cloth, and I had to squint to see the seams. I glanced at Isabel once. During the morning and early afternoon, the man with the white hair didn't come near me. Then, through the sides of my eyes, I saw him cross the room and move behind me. "Get up and come with me," he said.

I panicked and looked at Alicia. Her face was white and she started to get up. "Now!" he ordered. I pushed my chair back, my heart pounding, and followed him into a little hall behind the main room, out of sight of the other women. The man laughed and grabbed me by my shoulders, and as I twisted to get away from him, he snarled, "You're illegal. I can do anything." He laughed

52

again, and I smelled the Guardias and saw the blood as he reached for my breast.

I screamed, "Stop! Don't!" and swung out hard with my fist, smashing him in the nose. He slapped me across my face, but I twisted away and kicked him in the leg and screamed, "Stay away!"

I ran through the other room. Alicia threw my coat at me, and I saw Isabel and the other women cluster by the door to the back hall, making it hard for the man to follow me. I slammed out the sewing-room door, practically fell down the steps, and ran out of the building into the cold. Finally, I stood, shivering and shaking, waiting for the El. We had almost no food, I thought, little money, and now I didn't have work and wouldn't be paid.

Oscar was lying on our mattress when I got back to our room, and he looked up at me without much interest. Julia was away, washing dishes. Only the harmonica man was home, and he played sad, faraway music. Outside the window, the sun was low in the sky, and its reflection glowed on a few high windows. The rest of the buildings were in shadows. I sat down, my back against the wall, and rested.

Someone knocked on our apartment door, and the harmonica man quit playing and went to it. I heard low voices in Spanish; then Tomás stepped into our doorway.

"I came to see if you or Julia were here," he said. "They've begun feeding people at one of the churches, the one where Marta got your clothes. They don't check to see if you're legal or ask any questions. You just get in line, and they give you something to eat inside. I thought maybe you didn't have food."

Feeling tears in my eyes, I looked directly at him and

didn't turn away. "Yes. We're hungry." I swallowed and nodded. "Are you sure it's safe?"

"Yes, I went last night. They didn't ask any questions, and there were other families, some like us. Bring Oscar and I'll take you there."

I stood Oscar up and put his coat on him. He seemed so thin and tired. Tomás asked, "Is there something else for him to wear? It might be a long wait outside."

I glanced around. "I don't know what."

Tomás looked up at our curtains. "Let's take one of those. We can wrap it around him." I got a chair and unpinned the curtain, heavy white material decorated with faded red roses.

As Tomás led us down several blocks to the church, I noticed he was no longer limping. His foot must have been better. It was dusk when we arrived, and a line was waiting outside for the church to open. We went to the end of the line and wrapped Oscar in the curtain. He looked so small and strange.

Tomás twisted the button of his coat between two fingers. "What happened with your job?" he asked me, tipping his head slightly. "Why were you home when Alicia wasn't?"

I stared down. "The boss didn't want me there any longer," I whispered.

"I'm sorry," Tomás said, and he blew on his hands to warm them.

I thought of Tomás's eyes. When I'd looked directly at them, they looked deep, like I imagined the ocean.

The little girl in front of me cried, and her mother picked her up and tried to soothe her in Spanish. A pregnant blonde woman joined the line behind us. Her nose was red, and she didn't seem to have any eyelashes. Then an old woman hobbled over to us, pushing a tattered baby buggy stuffed with newspapers, plastic flowers, and empty cans. She walked stiffly, with short, quick steps, staring straight ahead and wearing a ragged red coat that was wrapped in a golden-green shawl, the color of the quetzal's wings.

She stopped in front of us, suddenly seemed to spot Oscar, and let go of her buggy. Her face was dark and wrinkled, and the upper lids of her large, weary eyes seemed thick with age. "Now ain't you a queer one," she said in Spanish, peering into Oscar's eyes.

Oscar blinked and stared directly back at her from the folds of the old curtain. I stepped over to push her away from Oscar, and she turned to me, smiling. Her chin jutted out, and her black hair was twisted into a rubber band and stuck straight out on one side of her head. Her eyes seemed strange, but kind. "You're in charge of him, are you, dearie? Well, the boy looks like my baby brother. Only one I ever loved. Sweet as sugar cane."

Tomás stepped behind Oscar, his hands on Oscar's shoulders.

The old woman continued to talk in my direction. "When you see me, you see my daddy. Look like him and got his ways too. Cussedness." Her eyes squinted, and she jabbed a long gnarled finger at the air. "I just the very devil, me." Then her eyes turned soft, and she reached out to pat Oscar. "But not my baby brother."

Oscar's face grew sober. "Have you seen the shadow man?" he asked clearly.

"Many a time, many a time," she said, and she crossed herself, pulled a cross with Jesus on it from her pocket, and held it in front of Oscar. "Take this, *mijito*," she said. "It'll keep you safe." Oscar reached up from the folds of the curtain and clutched the cross. His eyes glowed.

"When the weather's better, you can visit me," she said. "I'll teach you to feed pigeons." She bent down and whispered close to his ear. "See, if you're very clever, sometimes you can steal a little bread." She nodded toward the church and smiled. Oscar giggled.

"Well, well, the boy's better off," the old woman sighed. She stood back up and slapped her hands several times against her side. Even in the near dark, I thought I saw dust rise from her coat. "We must be about our work, mustn't we?" she spoke to the empty air behind her shoulder. "Doggone right," she said, as if in response. "Take care of your own, and God'll take care of the others." She gave a courtly bow at the air, then turned to me and winked. "I got funny ways," she said as she left, pushing her buggy to the end of the line.

I looked at Tomás, trying not to laugh. "Where did she come from?" I asked.

"Damned if I know." Tomás laughed as he arched his eyebrows, shrugged his shoulders, and gestured upward with his hands.

Oscar tugged on my sleeve. "Her shawl, it's the color of the quetzal bird in the cage," he said. I nodded, staring after her and remembering how I'd freed the bird.

"That's right. You talked about it in the crate. I remember," Tomás responded. "You said you saw a quetzal. It was still alive? I thought they'd die in a cage."

"We found it in time," I answered. "Papá told us stories about them. He said quetzals are shy and like to live in forests, not around people." I pictured the thrashing bird as I'd worked to open the cage. Its brown-black eyes had seemed to beg for freedom.

"I heard the Indians thought quetzals stood for beauty. And goodness," Tomás said, and again I nodded.

"Magic. Don't forget the magic," Oscar added.

Suddenly, the church door opened and people pressed forward. I grabbed Oscar's hand as we moved quickly to the door. Oscar, Tomás, and I filled our empty stomachs with hot stew, canned fruit, and bread. Oscar fell asleep

56

smiling that night, and I promised I'd be with him the next day. As he slept, I wrote a letter saying good-bye to Isabel to send with Alicia to work in the morning.

As Julia and I lay on our mattress, I whispered, "Do you think it was all right for me to take Oscar to the church with Tomás?"

Julia reached over and touched my hair. "Yes, Little Sister, I think Papá would approve. And Mamá." I smiled, thought of Isabel, and fell asleep.

I found no work during the following days, so Oscar and I stayed indoors watching television most of the time. We laughed at the game shows, and I tried to learn the sounds of English. I told Oscar stories to keep him talking and wished we were at home so I could draw my pictures in the dirt. Oscar often watched the men playing cards, and when the man with the tattoo won, he would laugh, pull Oscar against him, and tousle Oscar's hair. Oscar would be a little shy, but he'd giggle.

Our bathroom had a mirror, and in the late afternoons, before going to the church with Tomás, I'd comb my hair in different ways, trying to look older. Sometimes I pulled my dark hair over one shoulder, sometimes I wore one braid down my back, but most of the time I wore it combed straight back with a ribbon I'd cut from the curtain. A few times I just watched myself in the mirror and sang Julia's songs.

Often I'd stare at my eyes. I was beginning to look directly at Tomás when we'd talk at the church. I was embarrassed that I'd do that. I didn't think Papá'd have liked it, and I prayed to Our Lady that she'd keep me polite. Then Tomás and I would practice our English, and before long, I'd look at him again.

One evening, as we were waiting with Oscar for the church to open so we could eat, I said, "Tomás, that first

57

day after the crates, in Marta's apartment, you said something about the ocean. That you liked to swim far out in it."

Tomás smiled. "Yes. Especially during storms. That's when the waves are huge. Although Mamá or Marta never knew about that part of it. They'd have killed me if they'd known." He laughed.

"Why'd you like to do it? Didn't it feel dangerous?"

"Nope. I never felt scared in the water. I just felt like I was all alone. Nobody wanted anything. Just me and the waves and all that excitement." He ran his fingers through his hair. "See, I never knew my dad, and my mom, she was always working. But she had big plans for me. Big. So I started swimming out alone when I was really little. When I was out there, I didn't care about anything. I just loved the waves." His eyes smiled.

I watched the other people in the line for a few minutes. When I glanced back, Tomás was twisting his hair with one finger, staring far away. "I never saw the ocean," I said, "but Papá told us stories about it. About how he went out on fishing boats one year. Sometimes I'd pretend clouds were waves. Papá said you could dive right into waves, and they'd go over the top of you." I giggled. "Once I jumped off our shed, pretending I was diving in the waves. Mamá was really mad at me."

Tomás laughed at me and I picked Oscar up. "When I was little," he said, "kids used to tease me because my eyes were blue. Then Mamá'd sing songs to me and tell me I had the ocean in my eyes. Guess that's why I wasn't scared during storms." I lay on our mattress that night and thought of Tomás swimming in the ocean.

The next afternoon the harmonica man brought home a stack of cream-colored paper. Words in English and a drawing of a raised fist were printed on one side, but the other side was blank. I began drawing on the paper with our pencil, and when the harmonica man saw my excitement, he gave me money for crayons and a few felt-tip pens like we had seen in the toy store. I spent the next days on my hands and knees on the floor, drawing pictures of home for Oscar.

I drew him a blue sky with a rainbow of all the colors rising above bright green sugar cane fields. I drew him the head of a green and white rooster, its shiny black eyes staring at us and its red comb crowning its head, while our dirt-brown dog stood in the background. I drew him a bell tower in a white church against a blue sky with a bird flying toward it. I drew him violet and pink lilies, and a pale yellow and orange butterfly rising into the air. I drew him the magnificent quetzal from Papá's stories, with its intelligent eyes, its golden-green wings and colored plumes, and its red-and-white body as it soared up into the sky away from the cage. But I drew no people for Oscar, even when he pleaded with me, "Please, María, draw Mamá. Draw Mamá."

I'd shake my head and say, "No, Oscar, I can't draw Mamá. Not Mamá or Papá."

When Alicia saw all of our pictures from home, she brought us a roll of tape, and we taped them on the walls of the rooms and especially above the mattresses. The men smiled at night over our newest work, and Oscar's eyes warmed with the pictures. Still, even with the food from the church, he grew thinner.

One afternoon, while fresh air blew in from our open window and I heard birds, Oscar slept on our mattress with his arm thrown over his face. I sat there watching his fragile breathing and felt fear deep within my stomach. I'd watched other little brothers get thinner, then get sick and die. Three of them as babies. And I'd never loved them as much as I loved Oscar.

I touched Oscar's pale cheek, but he didn't wake, just kept breathing shallowly. I trembled, not knowing what to do, then knelt on the floor next to him and drew him another picture. I sketched a little brown boy standing beneath a green *amate* tree, a tiny bird on his shoulder as he tossed pebbles into the air. I placed a house of sticks to his left. Using a pencil and brown crayon, I outlined the Virgin in the air above the tree looking down on the boy and colored in the Virgin's clothes with blue, yellow, and white. When Oscar woke, I gave it to him, and he looked up solemnly at me with tears in his eyes. "María, please," he begged again, "draw in Mamá, draw in Mamá."

I stared at him, swallowed, and nodded. I picked up the pencil and drew the form of a woman. She was stiff and lifeless, but Mamá. Beside her I drew baby Teresa.

Oscar reached for the drawing and knelt on the floor, folding the picture in half and pressing it carefully with his hands. He folded it again and again into a little square and held it against his chest. I felt tears on my cheeks from missing Mamá. From that time on, Oscar carried the drawing with him wherever he went, opening it up every so often, staring at it carefully, and folding it back up.

A few afternoons later, I decided Oscar needed some sun, so I led him back behind our building where there weren't other people. The snow had melted, the weather was warmer, and birds were singing. I looked until I found several little stones to give Oscar, and we bent down with our backs against the wall.

Pigeons flew from the roofs of nearby buildings and landed near us. Then I saw a red-and-white kite with a long yellow tail flying high above the roof of a nearby building. "Oscar, look!" I jumped up and shouted. The kite swept through the air and rode a breeze like a bird, then caught a downward draft and plunged behind another building.

As we stared at where the kite had disappeared, the old woman in the golden-green shawl pushed her baby buggy around the corner of the building. She jumped at seeing us. "Well, well," she said. "It's my little pet." She shuffled over to Oscar, put her hand on his head.

Oscar pointed up where the kite had been. "Oh, you saw the kite, did you? That means it's spring." She chuckled. "Spring," she said in English; then in Spanish, "Even the humble sparrow has its season." She turned to me. "Bring the boy and come with me, dearie. I'll show you the other sign of spring." She paused. "Those others. Wouldn't show it to them. No way. They don't know nothing," she said with scorn.

We followed her back through an alley and behind another cluttered building, where the old woman marched forward, breaking her way through the trash the way men at home would chop through brush with machetes. She looked at me over her shoulder. "House full of good kids. I's the bad one. Just be my baby brother that got along with me. To the others, I say, 'You done with me, then I done with you.' I don't go in with a lot of folks."

She stopped suddenly, straightened her shoulders, smiled, and pointed to the ground. Tiny bright yellow and purple flowers were blooming among dead weeds. I knelt down and stared at them. "Oh, Oscar, see. Like home." He peered at the blossoms and his eyes were warm. I looked up at the funny, frail old woman. "My baby brother," she said, "he thought flowers came from ribbons in the ground."

That night, as we waited in line with Tomás at the church, the old woman came around the corner, pushing her buggy. "Look," Oscar said as he smiled, *"La Señora Quetzal."* The Quetzal Lady. The woman's lower lip jutted out into a great, toothless smile. She pushed her buggy up next to us, bowed in front of me, then swept her hand through the air into the buggy, grabbed a bundle, and thrust it at me.

61

"Dearie," she said, "I brought you and the boy a kite."

I reached for it, delighted, and turned to Tomás. "She said a kite was a sign of spring."

He placed his hand on my shoulder. "When I'm not working, we'll take Oscar to an empty lot and fly it." The warmth from his hand spread through my back.

I smiled at the old woman. *"Gracias. Muchas gracias."*

A few days later, when the sun was shining and a wind blowing, Tomás showed up at our door. "It's a good day for flying the kite," he said.

I frowned. "I don't know. Oscar has a little fever."

Tomás went to Oscar and bent down to where he lay on the mattress. Tomás smiled and said, "Well, Oscar, you up to watching the kite?"

Oscar seemed excited. I placed my hand on his forehead. It was warmer than usual, but not hot.

Tomás looked up at me. "We'll wrap him in the curtain and he can stay quiet."

"Aren't you afraid outside during the day? Because of the police?"

"No." Tomás shook his head. "We look just like the others. No one pays attention."

So we wrapped Oscar in the curtain, went to an empty lot, and set him on some bricks. Then we put the yellow-and-green kite together and attached string. The warm wind blew through my coat, against my chest and up my arm, as I held the kite in the air, stretching as high as I could.

Tomás ran away from me, pulling the string. The kite flew into the air, suddenly turned upside down, and plunged to the ground again. "I think it's going to work!" Tomás shouted at me as he ran to the kite. He handed it to me and tried again. This time the kite swooped higher into the air.

Tomás ran farther, and it jerked up and caught the wind and soared. I stood staring at the sky. Somehow the kite avoided the buildings and lines. Other children joined us, shouting and laughing. Pigeons flew up toward the kite, the color of their wings reversing in the air as they swerved on the wind.

"Your turn!" Tomás shouted to me. I hurried over next to him, grabbed the string, and ran with it myself, tripping through the rubbish, but with my spirits soaring. The kite caught a downdraft and swooped toward the ground, but I grabbed the loose string, pulled hard, and ran again, and it lifted. I heard Oscar squealing and clapping his hands.

Tomás ran up next to me and placed his hands over mine. "Let Oscar hold it," he said, "before it hits a building."

We circled to Oscar, tugging at the kite to keep it in the air, but it swooped downward and hit the ground. Tomás ran to the kite again, held it in the air, and yelled, "Pull! Pull!"

I tugged hard on the string and ran. The kite went back in the air. I laughed with joy and excitement as I reached Oscar, who stood on his tiptoes, squealing. "Take it, Oscar," I shouted. "And pull tight!"

He clutched the string in his small hands and stumbled backward, the curtain falling from his shoulders. "Yeah! Yeah!" he shouted and laughed so hard he tumbled over. I grabbed the string and pulled, bent over with laughter until I fell on the ground with him. Tomás joined us and yanked the string, but the kite swept up, sideways, and fell. Out of breath and also laughing, Tomás flung himself on the ground next to us.

That night Oscar glowed with excitement, and I sat up late, working on a drawing of Our Lady I was making for Marta and Tomás. I'd sketched the form on a piece of wood I'd found. While the others slept, I filled in the

Virgin's figure with deep colors of red, blue, and yellow until the colors sang with the voices of our villagers at mass. *"Gracias,"* I whispered to her, smiling, before I fell asleep.

The next morning, in the dim light of dawn, Alicia shook me. "The man with the white hair is gone," she whispered. "I think it's safe for you to come back to work."

Julia was awake, sipping coffee and sitting on the mattress with her back against the wall. "I think you'd better go with her, María," Julia said. "Even though it means leaving Oscar alone. I don't know how much longer I can wash dishes." Her voice sounded like a sob. "I'll go to Marta's before I start work, to tell Tomás. God willing, he'll still take Oscar to eat without you."

"Will you tell Oscar good-bye for me?"

She nodded.

My cheeks flushed. "And will you give my picture of Our Lady to Marta and Tomás?"

Julia smiled at me. "Yes, Little Sister, of course."

A short time later, I rode with Alicia on the El. It was lighter now than when I'd gone with her before. The air was clear, and the sun was already warm. A good day for a kite, I thought and smiled when I remembered the day before. Still, I wondered if I shouldn't have taken Oscar outside with his fever. I also wondered how much Tomás noticed the darkness of my skin. Then I pictured the old woman in the golden-green shawl, the Quetzal Lady, and I smiled again and felt tears in my eyes.

CHAPTER SEVEN

So I worked with Alicia once more, but Isabel was gone. The new boss paid no attention to me, and I worked fast like the other women. Julia met us at the door to our apartment the second night. "Marta had a letter for us," she said, "from Mamá."

I knelt on our mattress, and Julia watched my face as I read from the penciled writing. "My dearest children," Mamá began. "The money you sent came and Teresa is a little better. With food and medicine. But we are in danger. More were deported, so I stay inside most of the time and watch Beatriz's children. I thank Our Lady that you are alive, and I pray that we can join you. May God be with you all, but especially with you, Julia, when your time comes near. Love, Mamá." I sighed, closed my eyes, and felt Julia squeeze my hand. Oscar leaned against me.

When we arrived home the fourth night after I'd begun to work again, Julia met me at the door. "We have to talk," she said. Her face looked pale. We went to our mattress, and she sat, her back against the wall.

65

"I felt so sick today," she said, "I took Oscar and went to see Doña Elena. She said that if I keep working and don't eat more, I might lose the baby." Tears rolled down her face. Oscar moved from where he was lying and placed his head against my chest. I held him against me.

"I can't lose it," Julia cried. "It's all I have from Ramón. But Doña Elena said I had to quit working." She was silent for a few moments, then sighed. "If I did quit working, I could go to eat at the church more often with Oscar."

She crawled a few feet to one of our boxes and pulled out two small plastic bags. One held herbs, the other pills. "And Doña Elena examined Oscar. She asked how much he was eating. She gave us *azafrán*, for tea, if his fever comes back, and vitamins for him and me." She held up the bag with pills. "But, María"—her eyes grew wide and she tried to whisper the words—"she says that she'll deliver the baby, but if I get real bad, I might have to go to emergency at the hospital."

"No, Julia!" I shouted out loud. "You can't. That's how Isabel's aunt was caught."

"I know, I know," Julia cried. "That's what I told Doña Elena. But she said we still might have to take the chance." Oscar clung to me and Julia sobbed. "I can't lose the baby. And we're not eating enough. What'll we do?" I leaned my head against the wall and felt dizzy.

After that night, Julia no longer worked. She just sat quietly on our mattress, sometimes singing or telling stories to Oscar. I thought maybe Oscar seemed stronger, with Doña Elena's vitamins. Most of the time, they did have an evening meal at the church, but they were often hungry.

I was hungry all the time too, and we had nothing to send to Mamá and Teresa. Alicia and I got paid on Saturday, and during the second week, we ran out of food

66

on Wednesday. Marta sent some bread, Alicia gave us what beans she had, and Tomás brought us some scraps he was able to sneak from the restaurant where he was currently working. Other than that, we waited for my pay.

I borrowed money from the man with the tattoo to pay for the El. I was weak and dizzy while I worked, and my head ached constantly. My mind began to wander as it had when I was in the crate. I remembered our beautiful processions during Holy Week, with flowers, music, and statues of saints.

Our new boss snapped at us when he gave us our first week's pay, but during the second week he no longer paced back and forth in front of us watching our performance. By Thursday of the second week, when I was eating so little, he didn't seem even to look at us but hovered by the door. Once a siren passed us on the street below, and he jerked back against the wall.

That Friday night I woke up screaming and drenched with sweat, my whole body aching. Julia held me. "You're all right, Little Sister," she whispered. "You're not eating. That's why the nightmares are coming back. Tomorrow is Saturday. You'll get paid. Then you've got Sunday off and you can eat. There's hope, María. Just hold on." So I fell back asleep.

The next morning I sat with my eyes closed on the El, rocking stiffly with the motion. I did not have the fare back home, so I would have to use part of my pay to return that evening. Alicia didn't speak, but laid her hand on mine. I knew she had not eaten either and had shared what food she had with us. She put her arm around me as we walked from the El to the sewing place.

"Tonight we get paid," she reminded me, "and you'll feel better. Don't give up, María. You're young. Your brother and sister need you."

Our boss was in a corner when we arrived, his back to us. We began working. By now I had realized that others were also hungry by payday. Most brought something to eat during the beginning of the week, but by Saturday only a couple had anything. I half heard sirens outside during the day, but by now the sirens seemed almost part of the wind.

Hours passed and my stomach hurt. Food, I thought. We need food. I noticed Alicia once when she was looking at me. "Tonight we'll eat," she seemed to say. Finally, through far-off windows, I saw that the rays of the sun were slanted low in the sky. Our boss slipped out of the room, but I kept on working.

Suddenly, the doors slammed open and uniformed men jumped inside. "Immigration! Immigration! Stay where you are!" they shouted. Screams crashed through the room as we jumped up from our machines. Tables fell over and women kept crying. I turned frantically toward Alicia. She shouted at me, "Hide! Hide! Under a table!"

Women were running toward the window and the back hall. I saw someone raise a chair to smash the glass in a window. Don't jump! Don't jump! I thought. The Immigration men came forward, and I stood, unable to move. Alicia slumped over her machine. I moved toward her, and she looked up at me and yelled again, "Hide!"

Turning around, I saw a table covered with cloth, crawled under it, and kept crawling. Cloth fell down around me, and in the dim light, I saw two other women hiding under the table in a different corner.

I heard the smash of breaking glass along with the screaming. Don't jump! Don't jump! I cried again to myself. Alicia! Where are you! The screaming, crashing of tables, and sounds of fighting turned to hysterical sobbing, like at home, when the Guardias took away friends and relatives. I heard a woman cry in Spanish, "No, no. Don't take me. I've got kids."

My table shook and a man shouted, "Out! Out!" In the dim light I saw arms yank the other two women from under the table. I sat rigid and silent, waiting to be caught, but the women didn't betray me.

I pictured Julia and Oscar on the mattress. There'll be no food, I thought. No food for us. Then I realized. Today was payday. The boss had planned the raid so he wouldn't have to pay us. Tears scalded my cheeks, and I burned with fury.

I stayed under the table for a long time, until the room was totally quiet. Finally, crawling out, I looked around. The room was empty. "Alicia, Alicia. Come back," I sobbed, running in circles. At last, I stopped moving and sat in the middle of the floor and wept. Alicia was gone.

After a while, I stopped crying and thought of the door. I yanked on the doorknob, but it was locked. I yanked and yanked, then kicked it hard. On the third kick it opened. It was dark when I got outside, and I remembered I had no money for the El. For a few minutes, I thought I would faint from hunger and exhaustion, but I sat on the curb and waited for the dizziness to pass. Feeling better, I walked toward the El station. No one was there, so I wandered down a street.

Even though the weather was warmer than when we first came north, a wind blew and I was cold. Three men stood on a corner. They looked at me, and I circled around them. I saw more men and several women who were by themselves, their bodies arched by a doorway. One was white, one was black, and I could not see the face of the third. Men walked up and down the street and stopped to talk with the women. Music came from car radios and doorways.

I was afraid and crouched back in a door so the men

wouldn't see me, but I was so cold, I shivered. When I squeezed my arms for warmth, a man noticed me move. He started walking toward me, swaying slightly, and called to me in English. I shook my head at him and started walking backward, away. He kept coming at me, calling to me, and I stumbled. "No, no." He caught up with me and grabbed my arm. "No! No!" I shouted again and twisted away from him, turned, and ran.

I ran down several blocks. Finally, I stopped and just walked. The streets were more crowded, music came from many directions, and orange and blue signs showed women with no clothes. Women stood alone or in small groups, laughing and calling to men. I was so tired and hungry, I felt faint again. Sitting down in a doorway, I held my head in my hands.

Then a woman's voice called to me in Spanish, "Hey, little girl, you okay?" She called to me again and I stood up. She had on a lot of makeup, her red hair was piled high on her head, and she wore so few clothes I thought she must be freezing. "You okay?" she repeated.

I went to her, tears on my face, shaking my head.

"What's wrong?"

"I'm lost and hungry and don't have any money for the El so I can't go home," I cried.

She looked up and down my body and back at my face. "New arrival?" she asked me.

I nodded.

She got some money out of her purse. "Get yourself a couple of doughnuts in there." She motioned toward a coffee shop. "When you come back out, I'll tell you where to catch the El."

I went into the shop with the money, blinking from the bright fluorescent lights, and pointed to some doughnuts and held out the cash. Several men sat at a table, and I felt their eyes burn against me as they examined me from

70

my head to my feet. I glanced out to the street where the woman stood. She was talking to a man in a shiny car and pointing in my direction. Again, I was afraid.

I swallowed the doughnuts in big bites and went back to the woman. She asked me where I lived and I told her. "I'll walk with you and show you the station," she said. She nodded back at a doorway, put her arm around me, and started leading me away, her high heels clicking on the sidewalk. She led me into the dark, and I felt very frightened. If I did not return home, Julia would think I'd been taken in the raid with Alicia.

The woman stopped walking at an El station and stood staring at me in the dark, chewing her gum. "Hard, isn't it?" she said. She pulled her little coat around her shoulders and looked down the track. "Especially hard when there's nobody to look after you."

I shuddered and wished I could see the stars. Papá, where are you? I thought. Then I heard the El coming. The woman handed me more money than I would need. Peering at the El with her made-up eyes, she said, "This is the one. Maybe you'll make it home all right tonight. God knows what'll ever happen." She walked away from me.

It was the middle of the night when I finally got home. Julia and Alicia's husband met me at the door. Tears ran down my face. "There was a raid. Alicia's gone," I whispered to her husband. He turned his face from us, and his shoulders shook with sobs.

CHAPTER EIGHT

The next day Alicia's husband went to a legal aid office to try to get news of her, but he learned nothing. He returned to the office daily for a week but got no information. We knew that she would probably be deported, sent home, back to the killings. Our apartment seemed hollow without her. Every night before I went to sleep, I asked God to keep her safe.

I looked for work constantly, moving from building to building, asking in Spanish and my new, broken English if there was anything I could do. I got several cleaning jobs for a few hours, and when the church had enough, we ate meals there. Julia's stomach swelled, but she and Oscar grew thinner. I thought, If Oscar's getting this weak in the North, what about Mamá and Teresa with even less food? Then Marta got a cleaning job north of the city and began to look for work there for me. We took care of Marta's girls when she worked, and she often went through the rich family's garbage and brought us what food she could. Whenever the men bought food, Julia and I cooked and served it to them and Oscar. Then we ate what remained.

Julia sat most of the time now with her hands on her belly, her eyes far away, but one afternoon I glanced over at her and stared. Her face had turned totally white, her eyes bulged, and she moved her hands frantically around her stomach.

"What's wrong, Julia?" I asked urgently.

"I can't feel it. It's not moving!" She began to shake.

I rushed to her and put my hand on her stomach next to hers, tears in my eyes. "Julia, no. It's got to be alive."

We sat in silence, our faces without color, our hands cupping her belly. Then I felt it. A little arm or leg slid from one side of her stomach to the other. Joyfully, I looked into Julia's eyes.

"Yes, yes. I feel it," she shouted. "It's alive!" She threw herself against me and laughed and cried, and we thanked Our Lady.

That night Tomás came over and the men lent us a pack of cards. Julia, Tomás, and I included Oscar in our game, helping him with his plays. Oscar laughed when he won. I walked with Tomás to the door as he left, and he motioned for me to step into the outside hall with him, away from the men.

When he stood alone with me, his face flushed, he brushed his fingers through his hair, and his blue eyes suddenly seemed unsure. I felt shy and looked at the floor. "I have something for you," Tomás said, and I looked up. He put his hand in his pocket and pulled out a small gold locket on a chain.

I stared at it and stuttered, "But Papá and Mamá, I don't know if they'd let me take it."

"Don't worry. It's not worth much money; you couldn't sell it for anything," Tomás sputtered nervously. "Just a little present." He pressed it into my hand, turned, and hurried down a few stairs. "I—I wanted you to have something pretty," he said, looking upward at me. His face still seemed strange, but his eyes were warm again, like the sun. Before I could respond, he went down the rest of the stairs and stepped outside.

Oscar was nearly asleep and Julia was next to him when I returned to our mattress. I didn't know what to say.

Julia patted the mattress next to her so I would sit down. "You look different," she said. "Did something happen?"

I sat next to her and opened my clenched hand. Never had I been so shy with my sister. "Tomás gave it to me. It's just a present. He said he wanted me to have something pretty."

Julia reached for the necklace and held the gold chain with the little heart looped in her hand. "It's lovely," she said.

"Would Papá be mad?" I whispered.

"No, Little Sister." She laughed gently. I held up my long hair, and Julia helped me fasten it around my neck. "Papá'd know how different things are up here. He'd be glad you have a friend." I felt warmth spread through my body. When I looked in the mirror, it was as if my neck had been touched by light. I was so pleased, my whole body was singing.

Tomás didn't join us at the church when we ate there the next night, so we assumed he was working. The next afternoon, we heard a knock on the door. The men were gone, and no one usually came at this time. Leaving the chain lock on, I opened the door a few inches.

Tomás stood there. My hand went to the locket around my neck, and I smiled and felt a little dizzy. "I just heard of another church where they give out food," Tomás said as he came in. He turned to Julia. "You don't eat there; they give you groceries. I could only leave my job for a few minutes, so we've got to go quickly. I can take María."

"*Gracias,* Tomás," Julia said.

So we hurried down the stairs and ran down the street. When we stopped for cars, I tried to talk. "I didn't get a chance to thank you for the necklace."

"Looks real nice," he said, his eyes smiling as he looked directly at me.

Dark clouds were building, and a wind began to blow as we hurried to a high-domed church I'd never seen before. When we got there, the line was long.

Tomás fingered a strand of his hair as we stood at the end of the line. "Is Julia doing okay?" he asked.

"I guess so. But she and Oscar don't have enough to eat. I don't know what else to do. I'm scared for them all the time."

"I understand," he said. "Not enough food at home or here." We stood close together in silence, our arms nearly touching. "I've got to leave now," Tomás finally said. "If I don't, my boss'll be mad. Your English is better. Try to tell them you need food for us too." He squeezed my shoulder. "Good luck."

"*Gracias,*" I said, my hand against the locket as he left. The wind wailed as Tomás turned the corner, and a few minutes later, it began to rain. I stood looking up at the rain, thinking of how much I used to love the sound of it as it splattered on the clay roof of our house at home.

The line moved over, against the building, but there was no protection. The air smelled clean and sweet, but we all got wet and cold. I closed my eyes, and when I opened them, I saw the Quetzal Lady in her golden-green shawl. She was muttering at the sky with a newspaper over her head and buggy. She looked around and saw me. "Well, dearie, it's you. Where's the boy?"

"He's home. I'm trying to get food for him and my sister."

She didn't respond to me but turned her face back over her shoulder into the rain. "Look at this little drenched sparrow," she said and started to laugh. "Well, then, for heaven's sake, give her some newspapers, you silly woman. . . . I am, I am. Don't rush me." She poked through the newspapers covering the buggy and tossed them aside, bent down, and came up with some dry paper. "Put this over your head, dearie," she said to me.

As I did what she said, a woman came out of the church door onto the steps. She opened her hands to the sky and shrugged, as if she was helpless, and spoke in English. I couldn't understand what she said, but the people in the line said, "No, no," and began pushing forward.

The woman at the door shouted this time, and I understood. "No more, no more. Gone." My tears mixed with the rain.

The Quetzal Lady watched the line break up, then beckoned to me with her finger, "Come with me, dearie," she said loud enough for me to hear her over the rain.

"No," I said, "I've got to get them to listen to me. I'll bang on the door."

"Come with me, you silly girl. I'll show you the secret way."

So I followed her in the rain as she shuffled along the side of the church and down an alley. "Rain like this could bring hail," she grumbled as we walked. "Hail be as big as hen eggs at home. Could beat the devil out of you."

The back of the church was surrounded with a high

fence and locked gate. The Quetzal Lady led me to where a low building reached out to the street. "Climb the fence here, follow the roof, and go down along the wall. They got a window they keep open to get air. Then you can just take a little food from the kitchen." She laughed to herself. "Full belly, satisfied heart."

"How do you know about it?"

"Used to sleep and eat here myself. Tickled me to stay inside. I's right there when all that holy stuff went on. Before I got too stiff. Had some good times back in there, didn't we?" she said back to the rain. "Well, well," she shook her hands like a fan. "Time to pass on the secrets."

"Don't others know about it?" I asked.

"From me? Flies don't enter a closed mouth," she answered primly, her neck high and her dark eyes disdainful.

She steadied me as I climbed up the fence and over to the wet roof, where I turned toward her.

"Well, bye for now, dearie," she said. "Got to get on with our work."

I followed her directions, the rain splattering against me, and finally came to a partly open window, which I pushed with the palms of my hands until it opened far enough for me to climb inside. I dropped quietly through the window into a dim and empty room and glanced around, wiping the rain from my face with the back of my arms. My heart pounding, I hurried down a hall until I came to a kitchen and looked inside.

The light was on and the radio played, but no one was there. I began opening cupboards, looking for food, but there was none, just empty plastic containers. Finally, in a drawer, I found half a loaf of bread. I grabbed it, pushed the drawer back shut, and heard voices in the hall. Panicked, I hid in a supply closet. Two women came into the kitchen, talking so fast in English I couldn't understand. Pray for us sinners, pray for us sinners, I said to myself. The women left the room.

I hurried back to the first room but realized I couldn't climb back up, out of the window, and I looked around again in panic. There was only the hall. Shivering from my wet clothes, I crept back down the hall and went up some steps to the right. At the top of the stairs, I slowly opened a door and stepped into the sanctuary of the church. My hand holding the bread bag dropped to my side, and I stared forward in awe. I knew there were churches like this in Mexico, but I'd never been in one. The room was enormous, and slanted prisms of light beamed down from stained glass windows. There was a carving of Jesus on the cross at the altar, flanked by candles, flowers, and flags.

I saw a large statue of Our Lady, standing serenely in a huge foyer to the side. She was held up by a carved angel, wore a red gown and a blue-and-white robe, and was backed by gold, like the rays of the sun. My mouth dropped, she was so beautiful. I walked toward her, my feet making no sounds on the carpet. Candles in wine, blue, and green glass holders flickered in front of her, and flowers were laid at her feet. Her eyes were gentle and peaceful, and her delicate mouth was like a pink lily.

"Oh, Our Lady," I said out loud, "you can make Oscar and Julia strong. You can bring Mamá and Teresa." I reached for a match to light a candle but saw a wooden box with an opening for coins. I looked down at my hands. Not only did I have no money for a candle, I was also holding a stolen bag of bread. I flushed scarlet under Our Lady's eyes and dropped the bread. Then I heard the voice.

"May I help you?" a man said in Spanish. I turned. The voice came from a tall, thin, red-haired man, wearing the collar of a priest. The blood left my face. "My

name is Father Jonathan," he said. "I didn't know anyone was inside here." He glanced down and saw the bag
of bread. I closed my eyes and felt his hands on my arms,
as if he was keeping me from falling. "Come with me to
my office," he said. I followed him into a crowded room,
picturing the Guardias and my arrival home.

He wrapped a coat around my wet clothes and motioned me to a chair. I sat down, empty inside. "Why did
you take the bread?" he asked, sitting down behind a
desk.

"We're hungry," I said, then stopped myself. "No, I'm
hungry, by myself."

"Where are you from?"

"Texas."

I tried to answer his questions, but he knew I was lying.
The blood came back to my face and burned me like
wine. Finally, he said, "Child, I'm not going to turn you
in. I'm here to help people like you. On my honor as a
priest, let me help you."

I looked up into his eyes. They were slanted and blue,
with no eyelashes, but they seemed kind. He had a long
neck, a blond-red beard, and was twirling a pencil around
and around with the fingers of one hand.

"Tell me," he said again, and he took off his brown-
rimmed glasses, wiped them with a handkerchief, and
put them back on. "First, where are your parents?"

I thought of Alicia and Isabel's aunt, sent back to the
killings. Then I pictured how terribly thin Julia and Oscar
were becoming. I glanced at him again, took a deep
breath, and whispered, "Mamá's in Mexico. Papá's
dead."

"Your father died recently?"

I nodded.

"What happened?"

"The Guardias," I said.

79

I saw Father Jonathan stiffen as he heard the term, and he wiped his forehead with his hand. "El Salvador?"

I nodded again. Stammering, I told him our story, but I didn't tell him where we lived and he didn't ask me.

Finally, he rubbed his hands down his legs as if in pain, took off his glasses again, and looked intently into my eyes. "Not everyone here agrees with Immigration. Or backs the Guardias. Some of us are trying to change things. To make it legal for people like you."

"You are?" I said, my mouth wide open. "Not everyone backs Immigration?"

"No, many people don't agree. We're trying to figure out what to do to change things."

Tears came to my eyes. I couldn't believe what I was hearing. Father Jonathan bent forward in his chair and started twirling the pencil again. "We help as many people as we can here, with food and sometimes medicine. But we keep running out of money." He paused. Tears were running down my cheeks. "But for now," he said, pressing his hands against the desk, "I'll give you some food for today, and if you come every day for a few hours, we'll pay you to clean." He smiled sadly. "And give you some food when we've got it. I'm only here part time, though, and sometimes I'm gone." He paused again. "There're so many people." He looked around the room, twisted his long fingers together, and cracked his knuckles. "I keep thinking, there just must be some better way to help people like you."

"Gracias," I whispered. "You won't turn us in?"

He shook his head and smiled gently. "No, I'll try to help you as much as I can. Go back and finish your prayers, María. You can use a candle. I'll go get some aspirin and some food for today." I went back into the church and fervently thanked Our Lady.

CHAPTER NINE

My cheeks were warm as I began to walk home. It had stopped raining, and Father Jonathan's help seemed to be a sign of the Virgin's blessing. Partway down one block, I noticed a store window. It was crowded with religious objects, and a brown-and-white cat with one ragged ear tiptoed through ceramic statues of the saints. The cat wound its way past the precious objects almost disdainfully and suddenly sat, licking a paw, its head twisted to one side. I giggled. For some reason, it reminded me of the Quetzal Lady. A hand-painted picture of a blond Jesus was propped up behind the cat. Jesus' forehead was creased, and his eyes were looking toward heaven. I could do it, I thought. I could do that painting. The one I'd done for Tomás and Marta was just as good.

I walked quickly the rest of the way home, thinking of my drawings, the aspirin, and my part-time job. When I entered our rooms, Marta was with Julia, whose face was flushed. I began to show them the food and aspirin, but Julia interrupted me. "Marta brought us a letter from Mamá and read it to me. Things are so bad Mamá used all of her money and sent Teresa north with strangers. They're supposed to bring Teresa to Marta's address, but they should've been there already."

I set the food down and reached for Mamá's letter. "I pray that I have sent Teresa with good people," Mamá's letter said. "I'm afraid, my children. Write me as soon as you have her."

Julia's eyes were big. "Mamá must be desperate to send Teresa alone."

I nodded, feeling dizzy.

We made arrangements for someone always to be at Marta's; then we waited. I watched the light outside our window grow dark and return with the new day, but there was no word of Teresa. I worked at the church three times as we waited, trying not to remember the stories of children lost forever after their parents sent them north. Once, as I looked at the Virgin's face, I thought, What if Teresa doesn't come? What if the Virgin doesn't care?

Finally, late the third afternoon, Julia returned home from Marta's with another letter. The people traveling with Teresa had been caught at the border, and Teresa was back home with Mamá. I leaned back against the wall with relief.

When I went to church to clean the next day, I was paid for the first time, and I told the Virgin that I was sorry that I'd doubted. On the way home, I stopped at an empty lot that was filled with rubble. Old boards with nails, bricks, and trash lay in a heap together, but yellow flowers bloomed among them. I started to dig through the trash, throwing objects to my right as I dug deeper. Gradually, I came upon a few boards the size I wanted. I crawled out of the heap and rubbed my fingers across their surface, deciding on three, which were smooth and worn just right. Smiling, I touched my locket and started home, feeling almost like skipping.

That night, as Julia told a story to Oscar, I worked on a drawing of San Antonio for Father Jonathan, using my felt-tipped pens. The saint in my drawing tenderly held a child of Teresa's age in one arm, and with his free hand, gestured toward the child's face, as if offering light. The next day, Father Jonathan praised its beauty and carefully placed it on his wall. I glowed with pride.

Again, I worked late. This time on a sketch of San Martín, in brown, blues, and greens. Then I posed Oscar in the middle of a couch, and as he squirmed in front of me, I drew *El Santo Niño,* the Holy Child's face with eyes like Oscar's.

The next morning, I returned to the religious store where I'd seen the brown-and-white cat. I stood outside, staring into the window, trying to get up my courage. The cat wasn't in the window. Finally, as I stepped inside the door, a bell rang, announcing my presence. It was dark after being outside and I was afraid. Then I heard the purring of the cat, and it brushed against my leg. I reached down and patted its head, again noticing the ragged ear. A man cleared his throat.

I stood up. The shopkeeper had a big black mustache and almost no chin. He spoke in Spanish. "Yes, what do you want?"

Swallowing, I answered, "I want you to see my drawings. I saw the picture of Jesus in the window. It was done by hand. I thought you might buy others."

The man laughed. "Do you have any idea how well known that artist is? You're just a girl, and you think you could sell anything?"

I nodded quickly and thrust out my drawings. The cat brushed through my legs again. The man quit laughing when he saw the pictures. He set them on the counter and backed away, but I saw him glance at me out of the side of his eyes, looking me over. "Ah, well, they're not bad," he said. "But people, they don't pay much for things like this. I'll just make a few nickels from them. How much do you want?"

"Five dollars apiece." I forced out the words.

"No, no. Too much." The man shook his head, his mustache swaying, and handed them back to me. "Way too much."

I stood there, not knowing what to say. "Tell you what," the man said, "two and a half for this one. Three dollars for the other. Nothing higher." The cat jumped from a chair to the counter.

"Three for that one, three-fifty for the other," I said quickly. The man nodded.

The cat meowed as I went out the door, the bell ringing again. As soon as I was out of the shopkeeper's view, I leaned against a wall. Me. María. I had sold my drawings! Papá, Mamá, you'd be proud.

The money felt warm in my hands as I showed it to Julia. Immediately, I began working on another drawing.

Each time I went to work cleaning at the church, I stopped in front of the Virgin and prayed for Mamá, Teresa, Oscar, and Julia and her coming baby. I also prayed that it was all right that I was friends with Tomás. At home Julia and I didn't talk about what might be happening in Mexico.

Now that we had more food, Oscar's color improved and he seemed to have more energy. One afternoon Tomás brought him a red toy truck that he'd found among some trash. We took Oscar out behind the buildings, where he made truck noises and played in the dirt while Tomás and I sat with our backs propped against the sunny, warm bricks of our building. Tomás's dark brown hair looked bronze in the light as he leaned his head back against the red bricks. I watched his face, memorizing his features. "The sun feels so good," he said. "Like home."

"What was your town like?" I asked him. "What did people do?"

"Well, it was right by the ocean. People made their living by fishing. The men went out in boats. And we had wide, winding streets that went up the hill."

"Was it sandy?"

"Uh-huh, everything was. The streets, the yards. But we still had lots of flowers."

"Did you fish?"

"I never worked on the boats, but I'd help when they came in. And I used to work with one of my cousins at his refreshment stand that the fishermen used." Tomás began to laugh.

"Something real funny happened when I was working at the stand a few years ago," he said. "It was down near the end of the harbor. I was twelve, I guess, and I'd never driven a car. And my cousin Pablo came driving up in this old, old gray Chevy. It was in terrible shape. I asked him if I could drive it. He said, 'Sure,' got out, and slapped me on the shoulder. So I climbed in by myself. It was still running, so when I got in the driver's seat, all I had to do was put it in gear. So I push on the gas, and the car's heading down the road straight to the waterfront. The road turns right before you'd go over the edge, but when it's time for me to turn the steering wheel, nothing happens. I'm still going toward the ocean, and the brakes don't work either. So I start yelling and go right over the edge, crashing down into the water." I watched him with my mouth open.

"It wasn't far down," Tomás continued, laughing as he talked, "and the water wasn't deep, so I was just bumped around, but the hood ended up in the water with the back wheels up in the air. I'd covered my head with my arms, and when I looked around, the water was up to my chest. I was surrounded by boats with fishnets and an old ship rotting on its side. Then I heard Pablo yelling his head off at me."

Tomás was laughing hard. "You should've seen the look on Pablo's face."

I laughed too. "What happened about the car?"

"Well, it was in awful shape to begin with, and I had to work for a month to pay off the owner, but that was the first time I tried to drive. Aunt Marta said it was like everything else I'd ever done." Tomás arched his eyebrows and shrugged his shoulders. "Always has to do everything the hard way. What can I say?" I laughed so hard tears came into my eyes.

"What do you think of when you remember the good times at home?" he asked me.

"Well, nothing as funny as that." I tipped my head back against the bricks also. "I remember Julia and me, when we'd wash clothes on the riverbank. Before she was married. The water was cold, and we'd go where it was clear and rocky. We'd start off working hard, but before long I'd wade in and start to splash her. Then she'd splash me back." I began to giggle again. "Then we'd forget about the clothes and just start playing." I pictured sparkling water coming at me, Julia behind it, laughing and teasing me, the sun silhouetting her wet dress against her body.

"Mamá had a way of joking about us," I said. "A saying she'd use when we'd do things like get wet. Mamá'd look up at heaven and say, 'How could I get such daughters? Less help than two scrawny turkeys hatched from the same lopsided egg.' She'd laugh; but she never got too mad."

Tomás laughed. "Anything else?" he asked.

"Uh-huh," I said. "Not funny, but special." Oscar quit playing with his truck and came and leaned against me. "I worked a stick loose in our house, right by where I slept," I said. "That way I could see a little of the sky at night. Each night, when I was supposed to be sleeping, our neighbor played the *pita*, the wooden whistle."

Tomás nodded. "Yeah, I've heard it."

"Well, you know how the stars move across the sky at night." Tomás nodded again. "See, I always thought I had a special star, ever since I was little. And when our neighbor played his *pita* each night, my star would move right where I could see it through my crack. Then it'd move away. But it always came back the next night."

We heard a clattering, quit talking, and turned to see the Quetzal Lady pushing her buggy as she came to join us behind the building. She wore a torn cotton dress and tattered bedroom slippers. We stood up, she smiled her toothless grin, and she patted Oscar on the head. I noticed newspapers moving in her buggy.

"Guess what we brought you this time, my little pet," she said, bending in a stiff bow toward Oscar. "My baby brother's favorite." She began to dig through her buggy, tossing aluminum cans on the ground. " 'Course he liked damn dogs too," she said, looking at me. "I never liked them and never will."

She pulled out an orange kitten with a white ring around one of its eyes. The kitten meowed as Oscar reached for it with both hands and pulled it against his face and chest. The small cat stretched its forelegs out straight against Oscar's chest, staring directly into Oscar's delighted eyes. It thrust its face forward into Oscar's cheek, burrowing against him and purring loudly.

"Kitty, kitty, kitty." Oscar laughed, and the kitten pulled back from Oscar's face and climbed up onto his shoulder. Perched grandly, it leisurely looked us over, then rammed its nose against Oscar's head and licked him in the ear. Oscar giggled so hard, he almost fell over, and the kitten dropped to the ground. I knelt down, the kitten came to me, and Tomás bent against me. I remembered the cat with the ragged ear in the store where I'd sold my drawings. I thought, Maybe cats are lucky for me.

We played with the kitten, out behind the building, while the Quetzal Lady watched over us and smiled proudly. Finally, she said, "It's time for us to be about our work again." She gently took the kitten from Oscar. "But we'll be back some special day, just when you need us." She grinned, put the kitten into the buggy, and pushed it away. Oscar waved at the Quetzal Lady as she left.

CHAPTER TEN

One night, in the darkness shortly before dawn, Julia shook me. "María," she whispered, "my water broke, and the pains have started."

I opened my eyes, suddenly awake. "It's coming? But Doña Elena says it's not quite ready."

"But it's happening." Her eyes were wide and her face pale. "María, I'm scared."

I stood up and helped Julia to her feet. "Can you make it to Doña Elena's?"

"Yes." She nodded.

We told the harmonica man we were leaving. He said he was not working the next day and would watch Oscar. I wished Alicia was with us. Julia leaned against me as we hurried through the dark streets, stopping at times when Julia had a pain. We slowly worked our way up the stairs to Doña Elena's apartment. I knocked on the door. Finally, it was opened. I bowed my head in respect. "The baby's coming," I said.

Doña Elena glanced at Julia's stomach. "Come in and sit down," she said. "I'll change my clothes." She moved swiftly to straighten the blankets on the bed in which she had been sleeping, folded a towel onto a chair, motioned Julia to it, and stepped out of the room. Julia lowered herself into the rocking chair, and I sat on the edge of the bed, my body stiff with fear. Julia's skin seemed almost white in the night. She trembled and was praying.

Doña Elena came back into the room, wearing a dark print dress and a white apron. She went directly to her dresser, lit a candle in front of a statue of Our Lady, and whispered prayers. Turning to Julia, she said, "Come into the delivery room and I'll check you." She looked at me. "Wait out here for now, María, but your sister'll probably need you during the delivery."

My stomach twisted with fear, but I gazed around the room in wonder as I waited. Only in church had I seen such beauty. On one dresser, I saw lace, framed pictures, statues of Our Lady and the saints, and the flickering candle. An old wooden carving like I'd never seen before was placed on another dresser across the room. A little man with a blue hat and blue clothing stood in a stall, holding a staff in one hand, his other hand open toward heaven, his whole body polished with age. Beside him was placed a carved bull, and above him flew a wooden angel, with a golden dress and uplifted hands. A tiny lamp glowed next to the small scene, lighting it with importance.

I looked at myself in a mirror. I looked tired, and while Julia and Oscar had grown more pale, I was as dark as always. I thought, Julia is the beautiful one, Julia is older. Why me? Why did I have to be the one who Papá thought would save the family? Then I remembered all the suffering Julia'd gone through, and I was ashamed.

I heard Doña Elena washing in the bathroom. "She's partway along, all right," she said gently, returning to the room where I was waiting. "But I don't like her weakness, and the baby's pretty small. If something goes wrong, we'll have to call an ambulance."

"We can't! She'll be sent back!" I began to cry. "My friend's aunt, she was caught when she tried to go to the hospital!"

Doña Elena shook her head. "That's a possibility, but it doesn't usually happen. Don't cry, María. She needs you, and you'll have to be strong. She's frightened. You've got to help her stay calm." The old woman peered into my eyes. "Have you ever seen a birth before?"

I shook my head. But I had heard births, heard the sounds of heavy breathing and of struggle. I remembered Mamá's delivery of Teresa. Papá was gone for the season, looking for work, and Julia, a married woman, was with Mamá and the midwife. It was night, and the crickets were crying as Oscar and I waited in the shed. Julia had come out to us earlier and whispered to me that it was almost time and I should pray. So I knelt, holding Oscar against me, fingering Mamá's beads as I prayed all of the rosary. There were sounds of hard breathing from inside. Then we heard the high, shrill cry of a newborn, the infant Teresa.

Now Doña Elena put both hands on my shoulders and spoke with firmness. "Act like things are okay. The baby's faceup, which will make it harder. There's a painting of Our Lady on the wall for her to stare at. Try to keep her focused on that." She turned. "Come with me," she said, "and hold Julia's hand."

So I entered the birth room. Julia lay on a high bed, a sheet draped over her body. There was a little bed in a corner for a baby, and a suitcase with Doña Elena's supplies. I saw a cross with Jesus, hanging above the bed. I looked away from it; it reminded me of Oscar's shadow man.

91

Doña Elena pushed a stool for me over next to Julia, stroked Julia's face, and said softly, "You're doing fine. Repeat some prayers with me." Julia prayed along with Doña Elena, and I bowed my head. But I couldn't pray.

Suddenly, Julia stopped praying, jerked her knees up, arched her back, and cried, "Ohhh, ohhh, Mamá, Papá . . . Ramón, Ramón."

Doña Elena looked at me. "Hold her hand tighter and talk to her."

I grabbed Julia's sweaty hand, and she clung to me. "It's okay, Julia. I'm here. I'm taking care of you. You're just having your baby. Don't be afraid. Doña Elena thinks things are fine." I sputtered out the words.

Julia stared at the ceiling until another pain began. She arched her back and cried, "Ramón! Don't let them take me. Don't let them hurt me. Come back. Come back!"

I turned to Doña Elena frantically, and she nodded once at me, her face stern. Turning back to Julia, I pressed my hand against her cheek. "Don't be afraid, Julia," I said. "See Our Lady on the wall. She's caring for you. Pray to her."

Julia looked at the painting and moved her lips for a few minutes. Doña Elena stepped up next to her and held a cup of tea to her lips. "Drink a few sips of this, Julia. It'll help, and I'll massage your back and stomach."

Doña Elena undraped Julia's stomach and rubbed it. Julia was quieter; then she began to groan and cry again. I glanced up at the unblinking painting of the Virgin on the wall. Why? I said to myself, why are you letting Julia suffer?

"María, I need you," Julia cried urgently. She flung her arm out toward me, reaching for my hand.

I grasped her hand and bent so my head was against her chest. "I'm here, Julia. I won't leave you. We'll take care of each other." To myself, I whispered, "Mamá, Mamá."

Time passed and I sat back on my stool, and Doña Elena sat in her chair at the foot of the bed. We heard a knock at her front door, and she said to me, "Probably someone needs me. Stay with her. I'll be back in a minute." She took off her apron and left the room.

I looked at Julia. Her breathing was shallow, sweat stood in beads on her face, and she stared at Our Lady and didn't seem to know I was there. I walked to the window, away from the bed, and looked outside. It was daylight now. The sky was clear, and two small trees stood between the building and the street. New leaves outlined the branches of the trees.

Julia had another pain, and Doña Elena came back to the room just as it was ending. She dipped a washcloth in a basin of water and wiped it across Julia's forehead. Julia groaned. "Shh," Doña Elena soothed Julia. "You'll be fine. You're safe with me. I'm going to take María into the kitchen now and give her some breakfast."

She took her white apron off and motioned me to follow her into the next room and sit at her wooden table. Glancing over her shoulder at me while she worked, she heated coffee and took tortillas from the refrigerator.

"Birth isn't always this hard," she said. "It's mostly 'cause she's so weak and so scared and has suffered so much."

Julia groaned again. Putting her apron back on, Doña Elena said, "Stay here. I'll be back." Julia's cries diminished, and I looked around the room, seeing a scale for weighing babies, jars of herbs on the counter, and drying clumps of plants hanging on strings from the ceiling. The room smelled like Doña Elena had smelled when we first met her the night we arrived in the crates. She returned

93

to the kitchen. "Your sister's opening slowly. I think it'll be awhile."

"But she'll live?" My hands shook.

"Yes, she'll live," she said with compassion. "I'll pour us some more coffee, and we'll drink it in with Julia." She moved a bottle of herbs from the stove to the counter. I glanced from the herbs to the plants hanging from the ceiling, then followed her back into Julia's room.

Julia looked at us, and Doña Elena said gently, "I'm with you, my child."

"Me too, Julia," I said. I turned toward Doña Elena, bending my head in respect. "Doña Elena, may I ask you a question?"

"Of course."

"You're not from Mexico, are you?"

"No."

"Then where are you from?"

"I'm from New Mexico, here in the United States. I'm a citizen."

"But if you're from New Mexico, why are you in Chicago? It's so far away."

The old woman brushed the palms of her hands against her dress. "I came to be with my son." She sighed. "When the old ones I cared for were gone." She looked down at her hands. "Now my son's gone too, but I've got so many patients, many without papers like you. I just can't leave them and go back."

Julia had another pain, and Doña Elena stood next to her bed. When the pain was over, I asked Doña Elena, "Do you miss home?"

She sat back down on her chair and pressed her white hair back from her face. "Of course," she answered. "I was raised in the grasses of the *llanos,* as a sheepherder, under the huge sky." She paused, then said, "Did you see my San Ysidro?" She left the room and returned with

94

the old carving of the little man with a bull and angel. "It was my great-grandmother's. It's very precious, the only thing left from my childhood."

"What does he do?"

"He blesses the land. When I was a girl, every May we had processions, with flowers. We carried our big San Ysidro around to our fields, to give them goodness."

"We had processions too," I whispered.

She put her hand on mine. "Then you know how beautiful they were." She smiled. "The saint's blue clothes remind me of the sky at home." Pausing, she said, "Here we're lucky if we even see a sliver of blue, and it's gray and dirty."

"I know," I said softly. "At home, before the Guardias, I thought the sky was filled with angels, so we'd be safe. Now I never see it, and here, even the rain is cruel." I began to cry again as Julia moaned. Doña Elena set the carving down and motioned me to stand next to Julia with her.

More time passed. Julia moaned and arched her body, and Doña Elena massaged her back and stomach. Other people came to Doña Elena's door, spoke softly, and left. Sweat stood out on Julia's body like dew on new stalks of corn. Once, when I moved close to her frightened eyes, she asked urgently, "Ramón? Ramón? Where is he?"

I held her hands tightly. "Julia, it's me, María. I'm with you. We're here with Doña Elena." Tears ran down Julia's cheeks, she dropped my hands, and she lay back, staring at the ceiling.

I sat down on the stool and closed my eyes in pain. "Mamá, Papá," I cried. "I want home. I want home."

Doña Elena came into the room and pulled her chair close to where I sat on the stool. She reached out and placed her soft, wrinkled hand on mine. "María," she said, "you'll learn that the goodness, the goodness you had before, it can't ever really go away. It's all inside of you. Your family, your home, your land, before the killings began. You can keep those things living inside. Like my son and family live in me. And the grass and the sky. I feel them every day. They're still part of me, and it'll be that way for you." She sat still, with her hand on mine, and again I thought of moss on the high rocks near our home.

Julia cried again, and I went back to my place near her head, as Doña Elena checked between her legs and said, "She's opened enough now. It'll be soon. Like I said, the baby's face is up. That's why her labor's been so hard."

Julia screamed and thrashed downward with her body. "That's right," Doña Elena said. "It's time to push. Push . . . push." Julia shouted and pushed, her face purple with effort.

"Push . . . push," Doña Elena said and again began to pray.

Then Julia shouted, "Ramónnn! Ramónnn!" I looked down at Julia's legs. There was blood, and suddenly a little body slid into Doña Elena's hands. My mouth dropped and I did not move. The world was silent, and all I saw was the little form. Then I heard the sound. A high, piercing cry, as if the baby were enraged. "It's here," I said. "It's alive."

Julia stared forward. "It's alive," she said.

Doña Elena spoke from the bottom of the bed. "It's a girl, a fine girl. Just small, but active. Thanks be to God." She prayed quietly as she worked.

I looked at the baby. It was wet with mucus and blood. Doña Elena was tying string around the cord coming from its belly. Then she cut the cord with scissors and lifted the baby into the air for Julia to see, one hand under the head, one under its bottom, like a priest holding up holy wine. Doña Elena's face beamed, and I saw tears in her old eyes. She wrapped the baby quickly in a blanket and laid it on Julia's chest. Doña Elena smiled, wiped her hands, and stroked Julia's forehead. "You have your child. And she's healthy."

Julia was crying, her eyes filled with joy. I cried also, staring at the baby, my mouth still open. The baby's arms and legs jerked, and its eyes clenched shut as it cried. It was alive. Alive. But the baby's skin was dark, as dark as mine.

CHAPTER ELEVEN

I watched as Doña Elena washed and weighed the baby in the kitchen. When Julia groaned again, Doña Elena said, "It's the afterbirth," and handed the baby to me. I stood in the kitchen, holding it close against my chest. The baby slept, but I placed my finger against its hand, and its fingers locked around it. Our skin was exactly the same color. I thought of Mamá and how she would love to hold the baby, her first grandchild. I thought of little Teresa and her birth just a season before the Guardias came.

I touched the soft hair on the baby's head and felt my chest swell with love and sorrow. She was alive, safe; Doña Elena would register her so she would even be a citizen. Then why? Why did she have to be so dark-skinned? She would know enough pain.

"Julia's okay now," Doña Elena called to me from the other room. "Bring the baby back to her."

I took the baby in to Julia and placed it against her. Julia moved it to her breast, but the baby was sleepy and didn't want to nurse. "Later, later," Doña Elena said softly.

I bent down to Julia. "She's wonderful, but I should check on Oscar and go to the church to clean. And maybe sleep." I was so tired my arms and legs almost wouldn't move.

"I'll keep Julia here for a few days," Doña Elena said to me. "So she can get some strength, and that way I can watch over the baby. She's small"—and turning to Julia, she said, "but healthy, thanks be to God."

I stopped to see Oscar and told him, "You have a new niece, Oscar Sparrow. You'll have to look after her." He smiled brightly. I fed him a tortilla I'd brought from Doña Elena, then went to the church. Father Jonathan was there when I arrived. "You look tired," he said. "Is everything all right?" His slanted blue eyes were kind behind his glasses, and I noticed that his blond-red hair had been cut, so his neck seemed longer.

I smiled. "I have a new niece. She was born a little while ago." He asked about the baby, said he was happy for us, and told me to go home and rest. They'd pay me anyway. So I went back to our mattress and slept until it was nearly dusk.

After Doña Elena let me in her door that evening, she sat back down in her rocking chair, closed her eyes, and slept sitting up. I walked quietly into the birth room. Julia lay awake on her side, rubbing the baby's cheek. She glanced up at me, her eyes smiling. "I'm going to call her Ramona," she said. "Little Ramona, Ramona." She caressed the baby's head. "I will be a sunbeam, and enter your window," she sang quietly. I sat on the stool next to her and stroked one little arm that had come loose from the blanket.

Julia smiled. "You were so much help to me, Little Sister. I don't know what I'd have done without you. I know it must've been hard for you. You're young; you shouldn't have to do all of this."

"It wasn't hard. You were brave. And you've got your baby. She's alive, and Doña Elena says she's healthy. I stopped at the church to thank the Virgin." I bent my head.

Julia looked at me closely for a minute. "What's wrong?" she whispered. "Something with Oscar?"

"No, nothing's wrong. He's fine. Everything's fine."

"María, tell me why you're unhappy."

"I'm not unhappy." I turned away from her; my eyes held tears.

"What is it? Is something wrong with the baby or Oscar that you're not telling me?" Her voice rose in alarm.

I panicked. "No. No."

"Then what?"

I started to say no again, but Julia cried, "What's wrong?"

My voice broke. "I'm afraid the baby's going to be dark, like me. She doesn't look like you. She won't be beautiful. I'm thankful she's alive, but what if she looks like me?"

Julia stared at me, her mouth slightly open. There was silence as she looked from my face, down to the baby, and back to my face. "I didn't know you felt like that about your color," she said.

I nodded, ashamed.

Julia focused her eyes at the wall behind me, thinking. As she turned back to me, I dropped my head. "You don't realize how good you are? You don't know how proud of you I am?" she said."You don't know how lovely you're becoming? How happy I'd be if Ramona looked like you?"

100

I shook my head, tears on my cheeks. "I didn't," I whispered.

"Just like you," Julia smiled at me and bent my head against her. I cried, with my arms around my sister.

Julia returned home with the baby, and we played with her for hours every day. Baby Ramona cooed, kicked her little legs, and when I'd touch her cheek with my bent finger, she'd turn to it with her mouth and try to nurse. Her hair was long, and we'd comb it one way or another. When we were in our apartment, Julia carried the baby tied against her chest and stomach with a shawl, the old way mothers sometimes still carried newborns at home.

I also kept looking for food and money to pay our part of the rent. I sold three more paintings, found a job washing dishes in a restaurant two nights a week, and worked at the church a few hours each day, often getting groceries from them. Julia watched Marta's daughters while Marta worked, but Marta was unable to find me a cleaning job like hers. Because she was nursing Ramona, Julia needed to eat even more, but we were all better off than we'd been before. I was so thankful I'd trusted Father Jonathan. When I could, I practiced my English and did sketches of the baby to send to Mamá. We received short letters back from her, assuring us that Teresa was still alive.

With the arrival of spring, the world came alive with people, flowing out from buildings in the warm weather. Children played on the sidewalks and in the streets, groups of boys and girls my age hung around cars and doorsteps listening to music and flirting with one another, and old people sat on ragged landings, staring at the activity below them.

One morning Tomás knocked on our door. When I opened it, he said, "Bring Oscar and come with me quickly. I've hidden something in back so nobody will steal it." My hand went to my necklace as I looked at Julia. She nodded. So Oscar and I followed Tomás behind our building. Tomás moved some boards, then smiled. He shrugged and said, "I rebuilt a wagon for Oscar and Marta's girls, maybe even Julia's baby." He flipped his curly hair out of his face. Beaming, Oscar climbed into the wagon. The wheels of the wagon didn't match, it was rusty and had to be pulled by a rope, but it worked. "Someday I want my own repair shop," Tomás said, smiling broadly. "That's why I'm working so hard on my English." I looked at him with awe. I didn't know people like us could own a shop in the North. "Let's take Oscar to the park," he said.

Tomás pulled Oscar down the streets, and I felt proud, holding my back straight, my face soaking up the warm sun. I'd washed my hair that morning and could feel it warm on my shoulders. It seemed as if my arms and legs fit together better than they had the year before. I looked over at Tomás and felt the happiest I'd been since we had left our home. We walked close together so our shoulders sometimes touched.

We finally came to the park. I nearly cried when I saw all the trees touched with spring leaves. It was like home, where there is a sea of green in the wet season, fog rising in the morning, and a piercing blue sky. Pigeons flew up and around the park, and I thought of the eagle we'd seen once in the mountains, soaring in the sky with its eyes scanning the brush and crops. The sidewalks in the park were laid out like spokes in a wheel, meeting as the roads met in the plaza in a village near my home. A yellow disk flew through the sky like a ball, from one person to another. "A Frisbee," Tomás said.

"A Frisbee," I repeated, as did Oscar.

We walked slowly and noticed a group of people gath-

102

ering in one corner of the park. Children's laughter was coming from it. "I want to see," Oscar pleaded, so we walked closer to the group. As we approached, we saw small balls being tossed into the air with a steady rhythm.

"A juggler," Tomás said with excitement.

Oscar got out of the wagon and edged into the group. I followed him, trying to keep my hand on his shoulder. A man dressed in tight black-and-white clothes and wearing black-and-white makeup on his face stood in the center of the people. The only color was the red painted on his mouth and the red balls he tossed upward. Oscar kept pushing forward until he was almost next to the man. Then Oscar sat on the grass, his mouth open and smiling. He stared up with amazement at the balls, moving his hands as if he was juggling. The man noticed Oscar's movements, caught all three balls with one hand, bowed down at Oscar, and touched him on the nose with his finger. Oscar giggled, and the man bent down, picked a bright yellow flower near his foot, and handed it to Oscar. The other children laughed and clapped. I glanced back at Tomás, who stood behind us in the group. When he saw me, he arched his eyebrows and winked.

After the juggler had moved on, Tomás and I sat together on a park bench, watching Oscar pick yellow flowers and listening to what Tomás told me was country music playing on a nearby radio. Birds sang, as if happy the winter was over, and a cat stalked near us, reminding me of the Quetzal Lady's kitten. Tomás smiled to himself and tapped his foot to the music. I looked up at the trees. The light glistened off the new yellow-green leaves, and the breeze seemed to make them dance. Then Tomás moved his hand next to mine so they touched, and through his fingers, I felt the warmth of his whole body.

Oscar came back to us and climbed on my lap, clutching his flowers. I took one of the round yellow blossoms

103

and tucked it behind my ear. Tomás turned so he could look directly in my face. "They're called dandelions," he said. "You look pretty. It matches your locket." I flushed and glanced down. *"Gracias,"* I said, but then looked up again, directly into his eyes.

Tomás pulled Marta's daughters home in the wagon that evening, and as Oscar fell asleep, I told him the story of the sparrow who sang out the colors. As I told it, the sparrow's song reached out with all the colors of the rainbow and touched Julia, Oscar, baby Ramona, and me. Then the colors went down the steps and through the streets to Marta's, where they wrapped around Tomás, Marta, and her girls, brushed against Doña Elena and Father Jonathan, and headed south until they finally reached Mamá and Teresa.

CHAPTER TWELVE

A few days later, Julia found work at night, washing dishes. We also cared for Marta's daughters, and I continued to work at the church and at other cleaning jobs. We sent all the money we could to Mamá and Teresa, and with the food from the church, we grew stronger.

We received another letter from Mamá, saying that Teresa was weaker, and we wrote and sent a little more money. As I sealed the letter, Julia looked at me, her face strained. "I just think we've got to get them here soon. I'm so scared they won't make it." She was finished nursing Ramona and laid the baby down in her lap. "I know what I need to do, but I can't do it."

"What do you mean?" I said.

She pressed her forehead with the palm of her hand, and I saw such a look of anguish, my stomach twisted.

"Julia, what are you talking about? What else could we do?" Ramona began to cry and I picked her up.

"Don't ask me," Julia said. "Pretend I didn't say it." She stood up and left the room. I jiggled Ramona until she was quiet. I didn't understand what Julia was saying, but I was frightened.

However, late in the afternoon, Tomás showed up at our door, excited. "I couldn't believe it," he said. "I just saw one of your drawings of saints on wood in the window of a different store than where you sell them. One was marked sold, and the other said thirty-nine dollars!"

"Thirty-nine dollars?" I gasped.

"Yes, yes, that's what the tag said." Tomás came in and sat on one of the couches. "So I went in and asked about them. The salesman told me they were done by a young woman who'd become an important artist!"

"Me?"

"Yes, you!" he exclaimed, shaking his hands in the air. His blue eyes were shining, and his eyebrows arched with excitement.

I stared at Tomás, almost unable to understand what he'd said. My work. Thirty-nine dollars. Money to bring Mamá and Teresa. An important artist. I might really be an artist. I sat down on the couch next to him, speechless.

After Tomás left, I searched for wood until it was dark. This time I'd make the store owner pay me much more for my drawings. The man with the guitar visited our apartment again that evening, and before Julia went to work, we all sang happy songs together. While Ramona and Oscar were sleeping, I wrote Mamá again and told her about my drawings.

The next day was sunny, and the sky was clear. In the late afternoon, Julia took Ramona, Marta's daughters, and Oscar out behind the building while I stayed inside to work on a drawing. They were still there when Tomás knocked on the door. I opened it, excited about showing him the outline I'd made on the wood. "There's a letter from Mexico," he said.

I took it and sat on the couch. "Julia, María, and Oscar," the letter from Mamá's friend began. "My heart aches to tell you this, but your mother has been taken. She's gone, sent back to your country."

I started shaking so badly that Tomás took the letter from me and stared at it himself. "Where's Julia?" he asked.

My mind was blank, and I couldn't stop shaking. A short time later, Julia was back in our room on her knees praying, and Oscar was crying. "María, lie down," Tomás said to me. "I'm going for Marta and Doña Elena." I leaned down on the couch as he placed a blanket over me.

Dizzy, I closed my eyes and thought Mamá was beneath the *amate* tree at home, calling up to me as I climbed the tree higher until finally I was alone in the sky and Mamá had vanished. I rolled up into a ball underneath the blanket and did not move, seeing the Virgin's eyes. They stared ahead blankly, like she didn't care.

Time passed; then someone was shaking me hard. I sat up and opened my eyes. Julia was kneeling in front of me, her hands gripping my arms. Doña Elena, Tomás, and several men were praying. "María," Julia said, squeezing my arms tighter, "the letter says Teresa's still in Mexico. With Beatriz, the woman who wrote. She can't keep Teresa long. We must get her."

"I don't know if we can," I said dully.

"Don't say that!"

"I don't know if we can," I repeated. "Maybe we're all going to die. Like Papá and Ramón, now Mamá. Maybe the Virgin doesn't care. Maybe she's just a lie."

"That's not true!" Julia shouted. "It's not true. It's not true!"

I turned away from her. "They're dead. Now Mamá probably, too."

Julia slapped me. I looked at her, and she slapped me again. "Stop it. Stop it!" she yelled into my face. Oscar flung himself against her and started screaming, and I saw Doña Elena take Julia by the shoulders to move her away.

I shouted back at Julia, "Mamá's gone. One by one, we'll all be gone. We won't make it!"

My sister seemed to quiver in front of my eyes, her hand still in the air ready to hit me again, but I felt tears on my face. Then Julia reached for me, and I threw myself forward into her arms. "Mamá, Mamá," I cried as she held me. "I want Mamá. I can't save the family. We need Mamá. Poor Mamá."

That night, the others had gone, and the men were all in the other room to give us privacy. Oscar's eyes were closed, but he gulped air in his sleep. I lay awake on the mattress, and Julia sat next to me, nursing the baby. Her face seemed wasted. "We may never know what happens to Mamá," she whispered and sat in silence for a few more moments. The only sound was the sucking of the baby. "But we can't stop hoping," she said, putting the baby down.

I began crying again. "I miss Mamá and Papá, Julia. I don't like to let you know how much. And Papá said I was supposed to save the family. Then I didn't get enough money to bring Mamá and Teresa. Do you think God's punishing us by taking Mamá?"

"No, Little Sister, God wouldn't do that."

"Then why? Why would Mamá get taken?" I sat back up. "She's always so good. She always believes so much. Why Mamá?"

"I don't know, María. I don't understand." Julia shook her head; then she looked down at her baby and over at me again. "I'll leave Ramona with you and go for Teresa. We'll just have to get the money to give Ramona canned milk in bottles."

I stared at Julia blankly and realized what Papá would want me to do. "No, not you," I said. "We could never buy canned milk. I'm the one who needs to get Teresa."

108

Julia's eyes became tender. "No, I can't let you, Little Sister. There's just too much danger. Marta and some of the men are looking for rides south for me. I'll go, not you."

"But you can't do it. Ramona's still too little. She needs you, we don't have money for milk, and I know more English than you do. I can read and write. I'm stronger. I'm the one who should go." Oscar woke and started sobbing again, so I pulled him onto my lap and rocked him back and forth.

Now the baby began to cry. Julia jiggled her in her arms, distractedly. "No, María, no. Think what it'll be like to travel with Teresa. Think! You couldn't even take her in a crate! Immigration would hear you. I've got to be the one."

My face and body burned. "Julia, I'm going, not you. You can't stop me. If you try to, I'll leave tonight."

"Don't say that!" Julia nearly shouted. "You just feel guilty because Papá said you were supposed to take care of us. Do you have any idea what it would do to me if I lost you?"

I became very calm. "You know I can do it better than you, Julia. And Ramona needs you."

Julia glanced at her baby and back at me. "But you'll both get caught. You and Teresa. We'll lose you both."

"No, you won't," I said. "We'll make it."

The baby quieted. Julia quit shaking her head and stared at me, her eyes locked into mine, searching back and forth for my weakness. But I was strong.

Finally, she turned her face away, sat in silence for a minute, and whispered, "Then you'll go with money. I can't send you without it."

I was puzzled. "How?"

"I won't tell you, but I'll be gone at night. You'll say nothing of it to Marta or Doña Elena or Tomás. Nothing to any of them, you hear?"

109

My eyes widened and my mouth dropped open. "No, Julia." I flushed like wine. "Not like that!"

Julia glanced around the curtain, and I pressed one side of Oscar's head against my chest, my hand covering his other ear.

"I should've done it earlier. If I had, they'd be here. Mamá wouldn't be gone."

"There must be some other way. It'll kill you!"

"Well, I can't think of anything else." Her voice cracked. "You're never going to ask me the details. Understand?"

"What about my drawings? I can keep working on them. Sell more."

"It won't be fast enough. I should've done it earlier. I just couldn't." She choked on the final words.

I didn't sleep that night, but lay awake on our mattress, watching Julia, who was still, but also not sleeping. Mamá's gone, I thought, and Julia won't make it. She'll never recover.

Julia had such dark circles under her eyes when she lay nursing Ramona the next morning that I wondered if her face would ever be beautiful again. Oscar whimpered on the mattress, and I fed him a tortilla as he lay there. My body felt so heavy, I could barely move my arms or legs. "Julia, I need to go to church to clean," I said a little later. She nodded without looking at me.

Feeling sick to my stomach, I walked through the streets to the church. As I pulled open the heavy church doors, I knew I had to get some money. The interior was dark and cool. I knelt and crossed myself as I walked past the altar into the foyer where Our Lady stood, serene and lovely. Again, I lit a candle and fell on my knees. "Our Lady, Our Lady," I prayed. "Please help us. Save Mamá. Help me get some money so Julia doesn't hurt herself so bad. Make Father Jonathan know what to do. Forgive me for sometimes not trusting you."

Then I said to the statue, "I've got to go find Father Jonathan now. Please, help him figure it out." I crossed myself and went to the office.

The blonde secretary sat at her desk and smiled when she saw me. I tried to speak to her in English. "Please. See Father Jonathan. Important."

"No," she said, speaking slowly. "He is gone, away, gone to big meeting. For two weeks. Can I help?"

I felt the blood leave my face and my eyes widen. "No, not gone," I said. To myself I cried, Our Lady, why won't you help us? "Father Jonathan?" I begged again out loud.

The blonde woman answered, "Gone. He is gone. Can I help?"

I shook my head, backed out of the room, and ran into the sanctuary until I could see Our Lady. Her face still stared serenely ahead as if she didn't notice me. As if Julia and Mamá didn't even matter. "Why? Why?" I yelled at her, my voice echoing off the walls. I ran around the sanctuary, trying to find something to steal, but everything was fastened down. Finally, I looked back at Our Lady. "You don't care about any of us!" I shouted as I went out the door. Sitting on the church steps with my face in my hands, I cried for Julia and Mamá. I was no help; I couldn't even think of anything to steal.

Finally, I looked up. The Quetzal Lady was staring at me. Her shawl was in tatters, she had deep circles beneath her eyes, and she was shaking.

"What's wrong?" I said.

"I've come to warn you, dearie," she responded, lifting her trembling hand.

"What are you talking about?"

"They say they can't see spirits, but I can. I'm scared for you, dearie." She reached for me with both hands.

"I don't understand."

"Turn to the wise ones. Don't be talking to stiff old

111

boards. And don't be running off in no fool's direction. You young ones can be dumb, dumb as shadows in the wind." I stared at her piercing old eyes; then I pictured Doña Elena. She nodded as if she knew what I was thinking.

I left the Quetzal Lady standing alone on the church steps, her tattered shawl draped around her shoulders. When Doña Elena opened her apartment door, I stood with my head bowed.

"Doña Elena," I said softly. "I need you to tell me what to do." She led me into her kitchen. I thought her face looked much older, as if she too had slept little. She handed me a cup of coffee and sat next to me at the table. I couldn't look into her eyes. "I don't know what to do," I said. "I'm the one going for Teresa, but Julia's going to get me money. She told me not to tell anyone how she's going to get it, but I'm afraid for her." My face burned with the fire of betrayal, and I stared at the table. "She doesn't know I came to see you."

Doña Elena wiped the back of her hand across her forehead, pushed back her chair, and walked to her kitchen window. She said nothing for a long time, and I was too ashamed to look at her. Finally, she sat back down at the table, laying her hands out flat and staring at them.

"I should've helped more before," she said. Her voice was husky and strained. "We've got to stop her. After what Julia went through with the Guardias, she might not recover from doing it." She sat quietly a little longer. "I'll sell my San Ysidro."

"Your San Ysidro? But you said it was your great-grandmother's."

"Yes, it's the most valuable thing I have. It's rare. There're almost no others. I had it priced once at an art dealer's." She sighed. "It's what I can do. I've seen Julia suffering." She put her soft hand on mine. "I love you,

112

little María. You and your brother and sister. You'll need all the strength you have to get Teresa. You don't need to worry about Julia too."

"*Gracias,*" I whispered. "*Gracias,* Doña Elena."

Doña Elena went into her front room and brought back the carving of the saint in a stable with a bull and angel. She set it on the table. The saint's body was firm and slim, as Julia's husband's had been, but his face looked kind and tired, like Papá's.

I looked into Doña Elena's face. "You said it was all you had from when you were little."

She nodded. "That's why I want you to look at it very carefully before I sell it. Sometimes I can still hear the wind in it and smell the grasses. And I want you to know them."

So I stared at the old carving, memorizing its details until I felt the wind. I stared longer and the herbs in Doña Elena's kitchen merged together. I smelled strange plants from far away and could hear children singing in processions.

"I'll come to your apartment later today with the money," Doña Elena whispered.

I thanked her, went home, and waited, thinking about Mamá and wondering about Teresa. Julia and I didn't look at each other, and when Oscar cried at times, I held him in my arms and rocked him back and forth.

Early that afternoon, Doña Elena came to our door. I glanced at Julia. She was watching me. Doña Elena walked over to Julia, whose face had lost its color. "I have some money saved," she said. "Three hundred dollars. Probably enough for you or María to get your sister." She held out her hand with the money.

Julia began to cry. "Are you sure, Doña Elena? We shouldn't take your money."

"Yes, I'm sure, child. I want you to have it." She reached for Julia and held her in her arms.

I stepped forward. "I'm going, Doña Elena. Not Julia."

113

Then I dropped onto the couch, dizzy with relief. That day I grieved for Mamá but thanked God for saving Julia.

I went to talk to the secretary at the church the next morning, before beginning my cleaning. "Are you okay?" she asked slowly, her face showing concern.

I nodded, then said in English, "I will be gone. Awhile. My sister get food, clean. Need Father Jonathan to pray for my mother." Tears came to my eyes and I crossed myself, then repeated the statement twice until the secretary nodded.

Pausing every few words, she attempted to talk with me. "Father Jonathan . . . trying . . . to find help . . . for people . . . like you. Big meeting . . . church people . . . to make safe for you."

She said it two more times, and I answered, "*Gracias.* Tell Father Jonathan, *muchas gracias.*" I thought, Hope for us? People like us? As he had talked about before?

Exhaustion hit me as I began to dust the sanctuary. I sat down on a pew for a moment, my arms just hanging loose. Then I stood up and went on with my work. Finally, I turned to Our Lady, but I couldn't look her in the face. "Thank you for saving Julia," I whispered. "Thank you, and I'm sorry that I yelled and thought you didn't care." I glanced up at her face for a second. It still just stared forward, her eyes not blinking, her mouth not moving. "Please don't punish us for what I did. I promise, I'll always believe." I backed away, but as the church doors closed behind me, I doubted again.

CHAPTER THIRTEEN

We waited two more days, to see if someone found a ride south. During those days, Julia asked me two more times if I was still intent on going. I answered calmly yes, that if she tried to stop me, I'd leave right then. I tried to explain to Oscar that I would be gone and would bring back Teresa, but whenever I tried to talk to him about it, he'd cry and hold on to me.

Tomás came with Marta to pick up Marta's girls the second evening. I told Oscar to go into the other room so we could talk privately. Julia, her eyes down, said, "María thinks she should go, not me."

Marta turned to me, "But, dear God, you're so young!"

"It's so dangerous!" Tomás said, running his hand through his hair. "And we haven't found any rides yet, and you don't even know the way!"

I saw tears on Julia's cheeks. "That's what we need to talk to you about," I said. "What if I—" I glanced at Julia and said it quickly. "What if I hitchhiked?"

Julia opened her mouth to speak, but before she could say anything, Marta cried, shaking both hands in the air,

"Hitchhike! *Ave María Purísima!*" She rolled her eyes to the ceiling. "Don't you know what happens when a girl hitchhikes? You're as green as grass!"

"Then what about a bus?" I glanced around. Oscar was in the doorway, listening.

"But a bus costs so much money," Tomás said.

"We've got it," Julia said. "From Doña Elena."

"Ah." Marta sighed. "She's a good woman. A gift from God." Julia nodded.

"Enough money for all the way down and back?" Tomás asked.

"I don't know," I said. "Three hundred dollars."

"That won't do it," Tomás responded, walking to the open window. "Not coming back with a baby. You'll need rides part of the way." He turned and looked directly at me, a curl from his hair falling down over part of his forehead. "And it's so unsafe. I've almost died crossing."

"I know. I know," Julia cried. Oscar came running to me from across the room, and I reached down to hold him against me.

"Tomás," Marta said, "we can give her our map."

"Yes, yes," Tomás answered, pacing around the room. "And I know somebody who will make you a fake card. He charges seventy-five dollars, and if they look close, they can tell it's forged. But if Immigration just glances, it'll work."

Tomás continued to pace around the room. Then, suddenly, his face lit up. He stopped and touched my shoulder. "I know," he said. "There's a town about half-way down in Illinois that has many migrants. They're people from Mexico and Texas who follow the crops. If you get that far on the bus, one of them might be going south. There's a good woman there. She took me in once and fed me for about a week. Her name's Ana

116

Aragón, and if she's not there, others might help you. And if no one can do it, you could take the bus again."

"Oh, Tomás," Julia said. "It'd be so good if someone could help her. I'm so afraid about her going all alone."

Marta put her arm around Julia. "I know what the waiting's like," she said. "Honest to God, it's almost worse than going yourself." Julia nodded.

I went to our mattress and got out my drawings. "Tomás, when I finish these, will you try to sell them at the store, the one where they sold my work for so much money? It'll help Oscar and Julia while I'm gone." Tomás nodded and smiled gently at me. Then he gave me the address of the men who would forge me an identification card.

By the next night, I had a card taped in plastic to keep it from getting wet, and Julia and I took Oscar and the baby to see Tomás and Marta again. We talked together in the kitchen, away from Marta's boarders. Ramona whimpered, Marta took the baby from Julia's arms, and Julia bent down and held Oscar against her.

"I've come to say good-bye," I said, looking at Tomás, then back at Marta. "And to get the map and give Tomás my drawings to sell."

Tomás reached for the two pieces of wood I held. "These are good, but the eyes are sad," he said to me.

" 'Cause of Mamá," I whispered.

Tomás nodded tenderly.

"I made this for you," I said and took another work out of a bag. On a piece of nearly white wood, I'd drawn a bright sun splintering through the sky. The light shattered into blue and yellow and danced on the sea green that I imagined was the ocean. The water and sky wove together like a sunset and supported a swimming child. I handed it to Tomás.

117

He looked at it. *"Gracias."* he said. Then he hugged me. Finally, he pulled back. "I'll get the map." His voice cracked.

He went into the other room and returned. The map was worn at the folds until it was fragile, like the picture of the little boy I had drawn for Oscar. Everything was in English, and I recognized nothing. Tomás pointed to a penciled circle. "This is Chicago." He flipped the whole map over. "And this is the border of Mexico, at Matamoros."

I swallowed. "The bus'll take you from Chicago to Onarga," Tomás said, tracing the route with his finger. "That's where you'll find Ana Aragón." His eyes were soft and moist.

Marta went to a coffee can and took out money. "I've got ten dollars. Take this," she said to me.

"And I've got twelve dollars," Tomás added.

"I can't take your money," I said to both of them. "You've already done so much."

Marta sighed, "Ah, child, you'll need it." Tomás agreed, and Julia nodded at me solemnly.

I thought of Teresa and whispered, *"Gracias."*

Marta reached over and cupped my face with her hands. "May God bless you, María. We'll watch Julia and the little ones while you're gone. One thing I can say, girl. You've got gumption."

Marta and Julia stepped back and turned away, pulling Oscar with them. Tomás reached for me, hugged me tightly, and held me against him. I felt his warmth spread through my body, then pulled back so I could see his face. I saw tears in his blue eyes.

"I thought of leaving the necklace with Julia, but I decided to wear it—for luck," I whispered.

Tomás smiled. "Yes, do. It'll remind you of all of us

and how much we want you back. Be careful," he said softly and kissed me on the forehead.

As we left the apartment, Julia said to me, "I'll take Oscar and Ramona home so you can say good-bye to Doña Elena. I won't ask you if you talked to her about the money, but if you did, Little Sister, I'm grateful. Very grateful."

A short time later, Doña Elena knelt with me in front of Our Lady and the saints and prayed. I looked at the Virgin with confusion and wished I had the courage to ask Doña Elena if she ever doubted. As Doña Elena stepped into her kitchen, I glanced over to where her old carving of San Ysidro had been. The spot was empty, and the little light was gone.

Then Doña Elena came back into the room and gave me a plastic bag with some baby aspirin, vitamins, *aza-frán* for fever, and a tiny sealed bottle. "There's some medicine in the bottle that will make your little sister quiet when you cross," she said. "But be very careful with it. Only give her one or two drops. Too much might really hurt her."

"One or two drops only," I repeated. Then I whispered, "I don't know how to thank you, Doña Elena."

As I was leaving, the old woman held my face in her hands, and again I smelled the moss and ferns. "May the saints be with you," she said.

I prepared to leave early the next morning, sewing most of the money and identification into the hem of my clothes to keep it safe and carrying the plastic bag with medicines in Julia's pouch, which I wore around my neck. I kissed Ramona as she slept, and carried Oscar to the door. When I set him down, he wrapped his arms around my hips and sobbed.

Julia spoke. "María, if you've got to hitchhike, don't

get in a car that only has men. And stay near a door, so you can reach a handle." She crossed herself. "If Teresa's very sick, buy medicine and get her stronger before you try to cross back. And remember, don't give up hope for Mamá. Maybe she'll escape again." She reached out and touched her forehead against mine. "Oh, I love you, Little Sister. Remember that we're family. You're not alone." Her voice broke and she didn't speak for a moment. Then she said, "May God bring you back to me." She smiled through tears. "Papá always said you were going to save the family."

I bent down to Oscar. "Oscar Sparrow, I'll be back. With Teresa. You've got our pictures on the walls to help you, and Julia'll take care of you." I held his little body against mine, feeling the fragile life within it. Finally, Julia picked him up and kissed me again. I went out the door, down the street, and took the El to the downtown bus depot.

When I arrived at my stop, I took the stairs down to the confusion, rush, and noise of the center of the city. Tall department stores rose from the sidewalks and displayed plastic models dressed in strange, elegant clothing. The sounds of traffic, of police whistles, and the voices of people rang together, and I was already afraid and wished Julia was with me. A strange man stood against a building, holding a microphone and shouting out phrases about God and Jesus and the end of the world. I walked past a woman selling flowers, the flowers' sweetness reminding me of home and Mamá. Two blocks later, rising above the crowd, I saw the sign of the Greyhound Bus Depot, with an outline of a long, stretched-out dog, rising toward the sky.

Then I noticed a lamppost with a poster taped to it. A child's face, almost like Oscar's, was on the poster, the face frightened and the child's eyes pleading. I went up

120

to the poster so I could read it. Part of the writing was in Spanish and part in English. The caption read, "Justice for the Salvadoran Refugees." I stared at it with my mouth open and read the smaller print. "Join us," it said, "so victims of the U.S.-backed war against the people of El Salvador, like this boy, can stay in our land legally and safely." Underneath the words was a phone number. I felt tears in my eyes. Maybe this had something to do with whatever help Father Jonathan was trying to get us. I crossed myself and prayed as I walked.

A window on my right was filled with radios, tape recorders, and televisions. I stood for a moment, watching the television screens. Faces were laughing, and a wheel was being whirled around in a game show. I took a few more steps, looking at it, and as I turned and glanced back at the street, I saw a dark-haired man gluing up a poster on another lamppost—a poster exactly like the one I had just read. A blonde woman stood near him, handing out papers to passersby.

I stood quietly, watching them. The woman tried to give papers to several people, who shook their heads and hurried faster. Then she noticed me. She went on with her work, glancing at me. Finally, she stopped trying to give out the papers, spoke to the dark-haired man, nodded toward me, and walked over to where I stood. "We're part of a movement," she said quietly in perfect Spanish. "We're helping people without documents, those who have come here secretly because of killings in their lands." She paused, then asked, "Would you like to read about our group?"

I nodded. She handed me a paper. "We're trying to change the laws," she continued, "to give a safe place for people like the little boy on the poster."

"Won't you get in trouble?" I asked softly.

"It's worth the risk," she said.

121

"Are there many of you?" My voice cracked as I said it.

"Yes, many," she said and repeated the word. "Many. Would you like our address?"

I nodded again and glanced around, wondering if police might be watching. She also looked around.

Turning as if she wasn't speaking to me but staring out at the street, she said quietly, "We're having a meeting tonight. You could join us."

"I can't. I'm leaving Chicago for awhile. But I'll be back."

A policeman walked down the street, and I turned back toward the televisions. A man in a convertible playing loud music pulled against the curb so that it was hard to hear. "Here's some addresses and names," the blonde woman said, her voice louder. "Contact us when you get back. We're trying to change things and help people so they won't have to hide."

"You think there's hope?" I asked.

She smiled. "Yes, at least some hope," she answered.

I took the names and addresses from the woman. *"Gracias,"* I said to her and the man. *"Muchas gracias,"* I said again as I walked quickly down the street. Then, just as I turned to go into the bus depot, I saw a flash of golden-green go around a corner. I wondered if it was the back of the Quetzal Lady.

As I stood in line, my heart ached from saying good-bye to Julia, Oscar, Tomás, and the others, but I also thought about the blonde woman, the poster, and the addresses. I would memorize what she gave me and get rid of the paper.

CHAPTER FOURTEEN

I rode south on the bus, sitting next to the window, trying to absorb the loss and change. At first, all I saw was city: brick buildings crowded together and people cast in shadows even though the sun was shining. My chest felt tight, and thinking of Mamá, I closed my eyes in pain. I slept for a short time and woke suddenly. The angle of light had changed in the window, and I saw the reflection of my face. The childhood smoothness of my cheeks and chin had vanished, and I saw a woman with dark shadows beneath her eyes.

I remembered Julia, beneath the shadow of *amate* leaves at home, taking a break with me from the fields. She drank from the *tecomate,* handed it to me, and arched her head back so her hair fell free from her shoulders. She stayed stretched back like that while I drank also; then she straightened her back, swept her hair forward and across one shoulder, and smiled at me. In the bus, I pulled my hair over my right shoulder and looked into my eyes in the window. They were as dark as a well, and at their center, I saw a shadow of Doña Elena. May God bless us and keep us, I said to myself.

The buildings now were farther apart as the bus droned on, and stretches of yellow-green grass became common. I saw new leaves on trees that we passed, and the grass and branches rippled with the wind. Hearing soft snoring from the woman next to me, I glanced at her. Her dark lips hissed like a kitten in her sleep. I smiled, thinking of the little orange kitten, and I wondered what had happened to the Quetzal Lady. Then I looked out the window again, and my spirits soared. I heard the tune of the wooden whistle. The intense blue sky stretched from horizon to horizon, and great gray clouds swept up from the rippling grass. Rays from the sun streaked through the clouds and touched the earth with light. We were out of the city, and I felt so happy. Oh, Oscar Sparrow, here you would feel wonderful, I thought to myself.

Sometime later the bus pulled off the main highway, up an incline, and stopped in front of low, flat buildings. "Gillman, Onarga," the driver said. I moved forward and stepped out of the bus. The bus pulled away and I was alone. A town lay off to my right, past the countryside, and train cars sat on nearby tracks. I was in the middle of a large parking lot with cars and gas pumps, and huge trucks roared in place or drove in and out. An American flag blew on a tall pole on top of one of the buildings.

I blinked in the bright light, walked past the cars to a window of the largest building, and looked inside. A pale-skinned woman in a bright pink blouse stood by a cash register, chewing gum and gazing outside. People sat at tables eating. The pale woman noticed me and her eyes met mine. I moved away from the window.

A tall man came out of the door, carrying keys. He saw me standing quietly against the wall. His eyes took in my face and moved down my body. I stepped back. Arching his eyebrows, he laughed and walked over to a truck. I moved back farther into the shadows and watched other trucks and cars pull in and out. Most of the cars seemed new, better than the ones we had seen in Mexico or near us in Chicago.

I'd drunk all the water I'd brought and needed to use the bathroom but found none whose doors opened to the outside. Finally, I opened the door to the main building and stepped into the dim light. The pale woman stood behind the counter, in front of a group of American flags. "Rest room, please," I said, but she didn't answer.

At the end of the room, a sign said LADIES, and I started walking toward it. Three men sat at a table next to the hall with the LADIES sign. A wheeled cart with dirty dishes sat near them. As I started to step into the hall, one of the men, fat with short brown hair, pushed the cart with his foot so I couldn't get past. Another man laughed and said something in English about Mexicans, and a third said "illegal." I backed up, they laughed again, and I turned and hurried out of the building. I glanced back at the window and saw the woman watching me go.

I looked around desperately outside, trying to find a place to relieve myself, but there was nothing private. A gravel road led away from the highway across the railroad tracks, and I followed it over a small incline, where I was alone. I climbed down into the nearby gully and squatted among the dead cattail leaves. The bottom of the ditch was marshy, and fresh green stalks grew among the dead plants. I climbed out of the gully, my heart no longer pounding.

Bright yellow dandelions, reminding me of Tomás, dotted the countryside. I picked several and saw small violet blossoms growing in little green clusters. I looked up, holding my bouquet. Birds were singing under the

125

blue sky, and I watched red flashes on a blackbird's wings as it flew across a field. I thought of red chilies drying in Mexico and the red vestments the priest sometimes wore over his black cassock. Closing my eyes, I felt the wind on my face. Except for the birds and the wind, it was silent, and I breathed deeply. On the horizon, I noticed buildings of a town, and far away, a dog began to bark.

A car came along the road, blowing up dust from the gravel as it neared me. I started walking back down the road toward the buildings, my face forward. Finally, I returned to the truck stop and watched the cars and trucks as they pulled up for gas.

Sometime later, an old car drove up to the gas tanks, and a Latino man got out. A young woman with two children sat in the front seat with the window down, and a Latino man and woman sat in the back with another child. I went to the window and spoke in Spanish to one of the women. "I'm trying to find Ana Aragón," I said. "Do you know her?"

The woman smiled at me. "Of course; we'll take you to her." They drove me down a back road, surrounded by fields in which bushes and small trees were growing. Latino men and women were bent over, working in the fields.

A little later, I stood in a dark kitchen of an old house in the nearby town. My eyes burned from the chilies cooking, and the woman talked to me as she ground out spices in a mortar with a pestle. I heard a train pass nearby, and a little boy chased a girl into the hot kitchen. For a moment, I saw Oscar in the boy, but the woman spoke sternly to the child, and they left the kitchen. A baby cried in another room where other children watched television. The woman's long hair was pulled back in a red scarf, and she wiped the back of her hand across her forehead as she worked. She had deep shadows beneath her kind eyes. "You're on your way south?" she asked. "You're young to travel alone. You're going to cross back over?"

Glancing down respectfully, I answered, "Yes, I've got to get my little sister. She's alone now."

"But it's so dangerous for a girl like you, by yourself. There isn't anybody else?"

I shook my head, tears again in my eyes.

"How did you get here before?"

"Nailed in crates," I said.

The woman stopped working and looked at me, wiped her hands on her apron, and motioned to a table. "Sit down," she said, "and tell me everything, and I'll see if I can help you."

So I told her about our struggle for food, getting the letter about Mamá, and Doña Elena selling her carving, but I didn't tell her what Julia almost had to do to get the money. My voice trembled when I talked, especially about Mamá.

Ana shook her head sadly back and forth. "It must be so hard. You must feel all alone now that you're traveling by yourself."

I nodded and almost began to cry. "But Papá said I was supposed to save the family, and I didn't get Mamá and Teresa up here in time. Then I started doubting the Virgin. She just stares ahead. Nothing ever changes. Maybe God's punishing me. Maybe it's my fault. Maybe if I'm the one to get Teresa, things will get better."

Ana took one of my hands in both of hers and said, "None of this is your fault, María. And God wouldn't punish you. You've all suffered because of the killings. Because you have to be secret up here. Because people are so poor where you live. Don't you see?" She was silent for awhile, sighed, and let go of my hand. She took several more swallows from a cup of coffee and

127

handed me a napkin to wipe my eyes. "We won't let you get caught," she said. "I'll check around to see what we can do, and we'll pray to God and the Virgin for protection."

"No, not to Our Lady," I said. "I don't think she cares about my family. Her face doesn't even change."

Ana sat in silence again, staring directly at me with her steady dark eyes. Finally, she reached over and put her hands back on mine. "There are those who care," she said. "I'll try to get you a safe ride."

That night I slept with three children in a tiny room of a house trailer in the country. The room was separated from the rest of the trailer by a curtain. A rosary, plastic flowers, a drawing of a wide-eyed child, and a print of Our Lady hung on the wall. The night was warm, so the window was open, and a little boy rocked back and forth in his sleep. I lay there, listening to the frogs and crickets. The air was cool on my face, and I was so grateful to be away from the city that I felt tears in my eyes. I thought, If Oscar could sleep like this, he'd always be strong. At last, I fell asleep and dreamed.

In my dream, an old woman in black led me up a path in the mountains of Guatemala in which we'd traveled. I watched the heels of the old woman's bony feet press against the spongy ground. Finally, after much climbing, we reached the high place she was leading me to, and clouds drifted around my ankles. I looked down across the green of the mountains, past the places where we had hidden, past an empty village where we had found bodies of Indians. The old woman turned and faced me. Now she was draped in white and blue, like the Virgin. I drew back in pain but couldn't turn from her, and I saw great wild quetzals in the centers of her eyes. The quetzals flew toward me, lifting their wings slowly up and down, soaring forward. I was afraid and stepped back, but again, I could not turn away, and now I saw that the quetzals were gentle.

Dizzy, I closed my eyes. When I opened them, the old woman's face was back in focus, her eyes were kind, and through the wrinkled canyons of her skin, I smelled the herbs of Doña Elena. With tears on my face, I pleaded, "Can you bring back Papá and Mamá? What about Mamá?"

The woman whispered, "There's more, child, more than you know." Clouds rose so I couldn't see her, and I felt myself floating. I heard her voice. "You're not being punished. I wouldn't hurt your family."

"Then why? Why? Why?" I sobbed, my face in my hands.

Finally, her voice came to me again. "You're not alone, María. You can feel me on the wind. I'll come on the wings of birds. When you cross the river again, I'll be with you in the churning water. In the early morning, you'll hear my calls." The old woman's face returned. I peered closely at her and saw a glimpse of the Quetzal Lady, but she stepped into the robes of the Virgin and was gone.

I awoke. It was still dark, but the birds were singing with early-morning joy. I lay there listening to them, my face wet with tears as light dawned outside my window.

I stayed in Onarga for two more nights as Ana Aragón looked for a safe ride for me. During the days, I watched children for Ana's friends who were working in the fields. At the end of the second afternoon, Ana came to talk and sat with me on a step outside a trailer. In the background a rooster crowed and birds sang. A little girl squeezed up onto Ana's lap, and I showed Ana a picture I'd done for the girl. A bird flew over a cornfield in my drawing, and through the leaves there was a sketchy outline of a tiny child.

Ana pulled back and examined me, as if seeing my face for the first time. She smiled, her approval reflected in all the lines of her face. "María," she said, "you have a gift. You're an artist."

I smiled and dropped my eyes. *"Gracias,"* I responded.

The little girl squirmed off Ana's lap and ran to join the other children. Ana's face became more sober. "Also, I've got news," she said. "I've found you a safe ride, cheaper than the bus, with one of my nieces. She and her husband and kids are going to Brownsville, Texas, to see my mother. They were going to leave next week, but they can go early for you. This way you can help them some with the gas."

"Will I put them in danger?"

"A little. But Laura's willing to do it. She and her kids are citizens, and her husband, Manuel, is legal. But he doesn't have a driver's license, so she's got to drive. That hurts Manuel's pride." She laughed. "You know what men are like."

Ana poured herself a cup of coffee from a Thermos she'd brought with her and offered some to me. I shook my head. She sighed. "I carry coffee with me because I'm so tired, and it helps my headaches. There's always so many problems, with the people. I try to help them and translate, but I'm just one person. And my own kids, they give us trouble. Ah, Mother Mary, life is hard." I nodded and glanced down.

"I didn't mean to make you feel like you're just another problem," Ana said, concern in her voice. "It's just everything." She sighed, then looked down the road and wiped the palms of her hands on her jeans. "What's important is that when the mothers of these kids get home from the fields, I'm going to take you to our church to pray." She tipped up my face so she could see my eyes.

130

"I understand that it's hard for you to pray after all that's happened, but you'll need God with you."

A little later she unlocked the door of a small white building in the main part of town. "We fixed this up so the people would have a place to pray and come together and get help from God. Often, that's the only help there is," she said.

The light inside was dim, but I could see a print of Our Lady of Guadalupe against red, green, and white curtains to the right. A statue of St. Joseph holding the Christ Child stood in the shadows to the left, and a large cross with Jesus on it hung at the altar. To the right, in front of Our Lady, was a statue of a Mexican man, bending his knee in prayer and looking at the cross. Then I saw a sign with carefully lettered words in Spanish. I squinted to read them in the dim light. Ana noticed me and said, "A nun made us that sign. She said it's God's promise from the Bible." Ana read:

*"NO MORE SHALL IT BE THAT AN INFANT LIVES BUT
A FEW DAYS,
OR AN OLD MAN DOES NOT FILL OUT HIS DAYS,
FOR THE CHILD SHALL DIE A HUNDRED YEARS OLD."*

I stared at the sign. "For the child shall die a hundred years old," I repeated.

Ana led me forward and lit a candle in front of Our Lady. "Let us pray for your safety, María, and for the safety of your mother and your little sister."

Early the next morning, I thanked Ana again and left Onarga with Ana's niece Laura Lucas, Laura's husband Manuel, and their three children. The kids were still sleepy and whined as they were put into the old car, and we began our trip south. I sat in the backseat, watching the scenery and wondering if Mamá was still alive.

Laura's hair was red-brown and fell in curls on her

shoulders, and in the sunlight it seemed to glow. She smiled easily, and when the kids began to cry or fight, she called back to them and threatened to stop the car if they didn't settle down. Laura's husband seemed grumpy and rode without speaking, switching the car radio from station to station.

We traveled like that through the day and most of the night, stopping only for a few hours while Laura slept sitting up in the driver's seat. The climate got warmer as we traveled south, and the coldness of Chicago seemed far away.

Late the second night, I rode in the front seat, talking to Laura and trying to help her stay awake. My eyes were heavy and kept closing. Suddenly, the car swung off the highway onto the gravel at the side of the road. Manuel jumped up from the backseat. "What's going on!" he yelled.

Laura jerked the car back onto the road and said, "I've got to sleep. I'm going to park at the next rest stop." The rest stop was empty when we pulled into it, and I thought I saw shadows of palm trees before I fell asleep.

I awoke suddenly to flashing red lights and the static sound of a police radio. "The Guardias!" I said and jerked up.

Laura whispered, "Damn," and one of the kids began to cry. My heart pounded as a man in a uniform walked out of the night over to Laura's window. "Highway patrol," he said. I saw the gun in his holster and pressed my back against the car door. He looked into the car window. "Identification."

Another patrolman appeared at my window, startling me, and I crouched back in my seat. In my mind, I heard the guns at home and saw Papá and Ramón begin to fall. I gagged and pulled on the door handle. The patrolman jumped back, his gun in his hand, and I threw up on the ground.

Laura said quickly, "We're citizens. Here's my license, but my niece here has bad flu. That's why we're stopped." She looked at me to see if I understood.

I nodded and began to gag again, hearing Julia scream as the Guardias pulled her to the door. I threw up another time, then turned to the patrolman. "Yes, I'm María Lucas," I said, "from Chicago. Go visit my grandmother in Monterrey."

Manuel leaned forward. "Manuel Lucas, Onarga, Illinois."

The children were crying, and I felt sweat rolling off my face. The first patrolman handed Laura's license to the second, and they talked in English too rapidly for me to understand. Finally, the first patrolman handed Laura's license back to her, and I understood the words. "Rest. Then go on."

"Goddamn," Manuel whispered as the patrolmen walked back to their car. Laura waited until they drove away, then started up the car. The children's crying quieted. When we were driving down the highway, Laura sighed with relief. "Holy Mary," she said. "They said they didn't want to catch whatever you had, so they let us go. It's a miracle."

I cried in the front seat and remembered it all. I saw Mamá, Julia, Oscar, little Teresa, and me hiding in the gully behind our house as the Guardias returned in a jeep to kill us. I remembered our little home as we said goodbye. Chickens still scratched behind it, the *amate* tree sheltered it in front, birds sang, and lilies bloomed against one wall. Then we ran and kept running.

I traveled with Manuel and Laura to Brownsville, Texas, where we said good-bye. In the early morning, after checking my money again, I began to walk across the bridge dividing the United States from Mexico. Already long lines of Latinos were waiting to cross from Mexico to their jobs and the land of the rich, but no one stopped me, no one asked questions as I crossed in the other direction.

The Río Grande River, flowing beneath the bridge, was pale brown and about twenty feet wide, with green, sloping sides of grass and weeds. It looked simple to wade or swim, but the current ran quickly in the center. I stared at a small whirlpool on one side and suddenly saw the face of the old Guatemalan woman in my dream, her kind eyes with quetzals flying forward in their centers.

CHAPTER FIFTEEN

As I entered Matamoros, I knew I was back in the land of the poor. Turquoise, tan, and pink adobe buildings and weathered shacks were crowded together against the blue sky; thin, barefooted children sold newspapers and candy; adults tried to sell food from pushcarts; men polished shoes; and an old Indian woman and two skinny children stood begging. I passed an empty lot where chickens ran loose, and a child without shoes held on to a rope tied around a pig. Children laughed, babies cried, music came from shops, and a gaunt-faced woman sat with her back against a wall, nursing an infant. I bought a roll from a cart, drank a bottle of orange *refresco*, and got on a bus going to Monterrey. As I traveled closer to where we had lived with Mamá and Teresa, my fear for Teresa became stronger and the loss of Mamá seemed more real.

The crowded bus broiled in the heat, and even with the windows open, we smelled gasoline. Suddenly, the bus jerked to a stop. Cars were lined up along the highway. "An accident," someone said. I stuck my head far

135

out a window. Two donkey carts were pulled off the road, a little girl was herding cattle with a switch, and a roadside shrine where someone had died was to our left. Finally, a group of people in front of us moved, and I saw a truck that had jackknifed.

A boy on the bus, about my age, wiped his arm across his forehead. "Goddamned heat," he said. I thought of Tomás and remembered how he hugged and kissed me before I left. I touched my locket. Closing my eyes, I felt the sweat run down my face. At last, the bus began to move again.

Later that day, we reached the outskirts of Monterrey. I got off the bus and found a city bus going toward the part of Monterrey in which I believed Beatriz lived. We traveled through crowded streets, much traffic, and people hurrying in all directions. Finally, I thought I recognized a bull ring and a brewery, got off the bus, and stood still, bewildered. I remembered the cement-block housing with its little lean-tos on my right, but the shacks of adobe, weathered wood, cardboard, and tin to my left did not seem familiar. Yet we'd stayed in such housing, and it was in such housing that I'd find Teresa. I longed to have Julia there with me. I'd never imagined I'd be coming back here alone someday.

I walked down a road of rocks. Houses, shacks, and little businesses came up to the curb, and cows, chickens, and donkeys lived in the spaces behind the buildings. Children worked and played everywhere. A parrot hanging outside in a cage called to me, reminding me of Guatemala, and a wagon of watermelons pulled by a horse went by.

Then I recognized the tall pink walls and barbed wire of a textile factory and knew we'd lived nearby. Our shack had been of tin, resting against an adobe hut that still had remnants of blue paint crumbling from its walls. Beatriz

136

Esqueda had lived in the hut, along with her five young children; her husband had left to find work several years before and hadn't returned. But Beatriz could read and write a little, and since Mamá'd watched her children when she worked in the textile factory, it was Beatriz who wrote us about Mamá being deported and Beatriz who was supposed to have Teresa.

I walked up and down the narrow roads, trying to find where we'd lived, and occasionally checking to be sure the factory was still in my view. I began to ask people if they knew Beatriz, but they shook their heads. The sun went low in the sky, and its rays turned the smog and smoke violet above the homes. Roosters crowed and dogs barked. Everywhere I looked I saw thin, hungry children. Dizzy and tired, I bought another *refresco* and sat on the stones by the side of a street, my head in my hands.

Then a little girl spoke to me. I looked up, but the haze from the sunset surrounded her head so I couldn't see her face. "Are you María?" she asked again. I moved so I could see her more clearly. "Mamá said we were to watch for you. But she's gone, Mamá is."

"Virginia," I said, "Virginia, is that you?"

Virginia nodded again but said, "Mamá's gone. It's just us. Mamá didn't come back." Virginia was Beatriz's second daughter.

I felt tears in my eyes. "Virginia, where is your mother? Do you have Teresa, my little sister?"

Virginia led me by the hand. We climbed over part of a fence, ducked under some clothes on a line, and finally stepped into the yard of a little blue hut with a tin shack at its side. There, next to an old tire, eyes wide and blinking as she stared up at the darkening sky, stood a tiny girl. "Oscar," I whispered, then, "Teresa." The small child tipped her head up to me. One side of her hair still held the remnant of a ribbon. When I picked her up, she didn't cry.

I stepped inside the little home. Four other children lay in the dim light; one was softly crying. I saw a dark drawing of the Virgin. *"Gracias, gracias,"* I said and closed my eyes. I felt Teresa's warmth against me, but she barely moved. "What's happened? Where's your mother? Don't you have any food?" I asked the oldest girl.

A light appeared at the door and I turned around. A young, heavily pregnant woman stood holding a carton of milk and a kerosene lamp. "Oh, thank goodness," she said. "Someone's come."

"What happened?" I asked the woman. "Where's Beatriz? Why is no one with them?"

The woman stepped inside, placed the lamp and milk on a trunk, and pressed her hands at the small of her back. "Beatriz was hurt at the factory. She'll be in the infirmary another five days or so. I've been doing what I could for them, bringing them some food, but I've got others." She sighed. "You must be here for Teresa."

I nodded.

"That's good," she said. "Maybe up north, she'll have a chance. Maybe someday I'll go myself." She glanced around at the children. "At least they'll have some milk tonight."

I set Teresa down. She lay listlessly on the floor. I felt her forehead, but it wasn't hot.

"They're just hungry, I think," the woman said. "Do you have any food?"

"No, but I've got some money."

"That's good, good. I'll give them milk. You can go around the corner and buy them some tortillas and melons. Tomorrow you can cook beans. At least they'll sleep tonight."

So I bought food and returned to the children. We all

138

slept together, and I held Teresa in my arms, waking up three times that night to look at her and make sure I wasn't dreaming. The next morning, I gave her a vitamin. My little sister's nose ran, her arms were thin, and her legs were slightly bowed, but she was alive.

I wrote Julia a quick letter, letting her know that I'd found Teresa. Then I went to the infirmary, where I located Beatriz. She lay there pale and thin, her forehead, one arm, and one shoulder in bandages, but when I stepped next to her, tears came into her eyes. "I've come for Teresa," I said, "but I'll care for your kids until you can come home." She reached her other hand out to mine but said nothing. "We're grateful to you for keeping her," I said. "Do you have any message from my mother?"

Beatriz answered slowly, "No, she'd just handed Teresa to me before they took her. She told them Teresa was mine. We only spoke with our eyes. I've been praying for her."

"Gracias," I said again, my throat aching for Mamá. "I have money for a *coyote,* but we can use it for food, and when I cross, I'll do it on my own."

"That's good, very good," Beatriz said. "But, María, you must not give up hope for your mother."

I went back to the shack, where Mamá still seemed so present. "Is there hope?" I said aloud to the walls. "Is there?"

Our money went quickly, feeding seven, but Teresa and the other children gained strength. Still, I felt guilty using Doña Elena's money without heading directly home. I gave the vitamins only to Teresa, and one afternoon, as I pushed the pill into her mouth, I vowed to myself that I would help Beatriz's children, but no matter what happened, I couldn't help any others.

Two days later, I was beginning to write Julia another letter when the pregnant woman who had brought milk the first night came to the door. "A letter's come to Beatriz," she said, "from a refugee center in Honduras."

I took the letter, barely breathing. The return address was just across the border from my country. "Mamá," I said. "Maybe it's about Mamá." But the letter was addressed to Beatriz. My hand trembled. I did not know if I should open it.

"Beatriz doesn't have anybody there," the pregnant woman said. "I think you should read it." I tore the letter open.

"To Beatriz Esqueda," the letter began. "I am Sister Joanne Thompson at the Chaletenango Refugee Center in Honduras near the Salvadoran border. I send you greetings and am trying to reach Julia Córdoba, and María and Oscar Acosta with a message from their mother." I began to cry. "I'm writing to you and to an address in Chicago to tell them that their mother is alive and with us," the letter continued. "She reached us safely five days ago and is in fairly good health, although she's gone through much. She's begging us to find out information about her one-and-a-half-year-old daughter, Teresa. Please send us any information you have and try to inform her other children about her safety. Thank you, and may God be with you."

I swept up little Teresa, holding her out in front of me, her surprised face above mine. "Mamá's alive! Mamá's alive!" I shouted. "Safe. Alive. Like Oscar and you. She escaped again." I swung the startled baby around in circles until my hair was flying in my face and Teresa laughed like me. Then, carrying Teresa with me, I went to tell Beatriz.

Later that afternoon, when I'd calmed down, I sat with my back against the trunk in Beatriz's main room and finally drew a picture of Mamá. I drew her soft, round face, the cheekbones standing out with age and sadness, the lines of her forehead reaching with gentleness to her hairline, and her long hair pulled back in a rubber band. And then, after sharpening my pencil, I drew hope in the center of her kind eyes.

When I finished, I folded the drawing and held it against me. "Mamá, you're alive. Someday we'll all be together again," I promised. I also thought of Alicia. Maybe she was still alive too. Maybe someday we'd see her. That evening I wrote to Mamá in Honduras, telling her I had Teresa and that we were heading north to join the others. I also wrote Julia and Oscar, telling them all the good news and enclosing the picture of Mamá.

Two days later another letter arrived, this one addressed to me. I opened it quickly. It was from Tomás. "My friend María," it began. "I am writing to send everyone's greetings and to tell you that we miss you. We're praying that you have arrived safely and are with Teresa. Ramona's smiling and Oscar's fine. We hung your drawing of the ocean in the living room, and when I see it, I see you. The Quetzal Lady seems to be gone. I saw Lake Michigan and it reminded me some of the ocean. When you return, I'll take you to see it. Be strong when you cross. I hope this letter reaches you. Your very good friend, Tomás." I smiled and felt warm, as if Tomás was watching me. That night I slept holding the letter.

At last, Beatriz returned, and I stayed for three more days to take care of her and the children. The third night, I said to her, "We need to leave tomorrow. Otherwise, I won't have fare back home. But I can give you a little."

"Yes," Beatriz said, "it's time for you to go. God has provided. I'll send a shawl with you to carry Teresa as you cross the river. Maybe when my kids are older, I'll try too."

"Maybe there's hope for us in Chicago, Beatriz. On my way to the bus, when I left, I saw two people. They were putting up posters. They said many people were trying to change things with Immigration, and they gave me addresses, for when I get back."

Beatriz smiled. "That's good. You've got to have hope."

Early the next morning, I put a rag diaper on Teresa, bent over from my waist, and heaved her onto my back, the old-fashioned way. As I did it, her little arms encircled my neck, like around Mamá. I stood up, tying her tightly with the shawl, and tickled her on one of her bare feet. Carrying bottled water and tortillas, I set out walking toward the city center to catch a bus northward.

CHAPTER SIXTEEN

Teresa seemed happy as she sat on my lap in the crowded bus that we rode toward Reynosa, on the border. She patted my cheeks and laughed. "Teresa, Teresa, Teresa," I said. "Te-sa, Te-sa," she babbled back, her eyes blinking. "María, María," I continued, pressing her hand to my chest, but she only answered, "Mmmma, Mmmma."

A little later, Teresa began to cry, and I gave her water and part of a tortilla. She sat on my lap, chewing it, drooling down her chin. As she began to fuss again, I put her face against my shoulder, rocked her forward and back in my seat, and sang a little of the song Mamá had once sung her:

> "The day when you were born,
> All the flowers were born too.
> The day when you were born,
> The nightingales sang."

It was hot and I was sweating when I finally carried Teresa down the steps from the bus in Reynosa. Men stood at the base of the steps calling out, "I'll take you north!" "Go with me!" "I'm a good man and don't charge much!"

A Mexican policeman walked past us and paid no attention to the men, but I was afraid. Shaking my head at the men, I said, "We've just come to visit Mamá," and turned away.

I carried Teresa to the plaza, bought us a cold *refresco* and a roll, and sat down in the shadows of a building with my back against the wall, watching groups of people talk in the afternoon light. There were mostly men, but also some women, and they spoke of crossing that night, both with *coyotes* and without. Teresa chewed on the roll, making nonsense sounds to herself. Then she picked up a pebble, flung her right arm back, and heaved it a few feet forward. She stumbled to it, picked it up, and threw it again. This time the pebble arched high and landed to her left. She picked it up and threw it a third time. It went up above her, and before I could grab her, it thudded down onto her head. She howled, plopped down onto her bottom, and reached her arms to me. I held her against me and rocked her back and forth. "Tesa, Tesa, Tesa, you're okay," I said, and she quit crying.

I thought about the river and the costs of going north. I remembered the terrible crates and how hard it was on Oscar. Deciding again it was safer to cross by myself, this time without a *coyote*, I picked up Teresa and moved closer to the groups talking around the plaza. Two women sat near three men. I walked over to the closest, a thin woman with short hair. "Excuse me," I said. "My sister and I need to cross. Can you tell us where?"

She and the tall woman next to her turned to us. "No babies," the second woman said.

"But we've got to cross."

The first woman glanced at the other. "No," the taller woman repeated. "The baby'll cry and we'll all get caught."

I tried to appeal to the first woman, but the second turned directly to me and said, "It's dangerous enough without a little kid. She'll cry and they'll find us. Get a *coyote* to take you."

"I can't. When we went before, they hurt us bad. And I don't have enough money. I'll give her aspirin and medicine to keep her quiet."

The woman sighed. "It's not safe like this, crossing with a baby."

"I know."

"Well, listen," the first woman said, "you can come with us to where we cross the river, so you know where the river's safest, and you can watch us cross. Later, if you still think you want to, you and the baby can try. But after we're gone." She glanced at the second woman. "Is that okay?"

The second woman turned to the men, then back to me. "They say that you can watch us if you want to, but we don't think it's safe for you. The water looks shallow, but there's currents and holes. If *la migra* doesn't get you, the river might. It's very dangerous with a little child, and there're bandits hiding who rob people and rape the girls."

My chin trembled, but I jerked my head in reply. "But we've got to cross. Please just let us know where the river's safest."

Finally, she arched her eyebrows and sighed. "Well, you can follow us, but your fate's in God's hands, not mine."

"Gracias," I responded.

I fed Teresa carefully toward evening. Then I said prayers, gave Teresa two baby aspirin and one drop of medicine, and tied her tightly against my right hip with the shawl. I also hung a cloth bag with food, two jars of water, and Tomás's map from my left shoulder. We followed the group of people outside of town and down a path along the river. Frogs and crickets chirped as the night grew dimmer.

At last, the group stopped, and the taller woman said to me, "Watch carefully where we cross. We will stoop down so only our heads are above water, but we'll be wading. The water's shallow where we'll go, but deep holes are on each side. See the rock across the river. Keep it in sight as you cross and try to stay to its right."

I nodded and she continued, "I still don't think you should do it, but when we get across I'll pray for you. Just please don't follow us right away. Otherwise, we might all get caught. I've got five children depending on me making it."

I thanked her again. Teresa whimpered slightly, and I rocked her in my arms until she quieted. As I watched carefully, the group slid down the bank and into the river. The tall woman stood up for a second, to show me that the water was shallow; then she crouched down like the others so her body was not visible.

I sat in the near darkness and thought I could see their heads as they crossed. Finally, it looked as if they climbed up the side of the bank. As I waited for time to pass, I prayed to Our Lady, forgetting my doubts and searching the stars for the Virgin's veil. "Virgin Mary," I whispered, "forgive me for being so mad when we thought we'd lost Mamá. Please don't hurt me by hurting Teresa. I'm sorry, I'm sorry for everything. Forgive my sins. Help us, Our Lady. Get us back to Julia."

I tried to picture Mamá's face and held tightly on to Tomás's necklace. Finally, I decided it was time for us to try. Teresa was quiet on my hip, and I slid down the bank on my seat, trying to balance Teresa and the bag.

146

I stepped into the water, clutching my sister, and saw the rock on the other side, visible in the moonlight. The mud at the bottom of the river was slippery, and I had trouble keeping my balance, but I lowered myself into the water, trying to just keep Teresa's and my head above it. She cried slightly when the cool water touched her body and reached her arms around me. I began to wade across, as much of our bodies underwater as possible, but I had trouble seeing the rock, and the current was strong.

I decided to stand up straight for a moment, to see if I could see the rock more clearly, but when I stood, my left foot slid on the mud, Teresa jerked in my arms, and the food and water pulled at my side. I tried again to stand, but I lost my balance, smashed my toes against a rock, and plunged myself and Teresa underwater. I thrashed my legs to find the bottom, but couldn't find it, and tried to kick my legs to bring us to the surface, but we stayed under. The current pulled Teresa out of my arms, and I grabbed for her in the muddy water. I felt her dress touch my hand and clenched it in my fist. The bag with water and food pulled us down, and I struggled to get its rope from my shoulder. Finally, I felt it float away.

I kept thrashing with my legs, but the water pressed against me, crushing my chest from lack of air, and I saw the old Guatemalan woman from my dream, the quetzals flying toward me in her eyes. Then I felt something firm under my right foot, and I heaved myself and Teresa forward toward it, until my other foot crashed into something solid. Now both feet touched bottom, and I jerked my body against the current, toward the surface. My head broke through the top of the water, and as I stood up out of it, coughing, I grabbed Teresa with both hands and wrenched her up out of the river.

I saw her face in the dim light, but she didn't cough or

147

move. I pulled her up over one arm and started pounding her on the back. Her head suddenly jerked, and she vomited. She coughed, gasped air, vomited again, and started to scream. I felt joy as I held her screaming in my arms, then remembered my pouch. It was still around my neck, so, stepping forward, one foot at a time, I waded back up to the shore of Mexico. We lay that night next to a tin hut, under some cardboard, crying.

When I woke up the next morning, I saw a young woman with dark skin and long hair in a braid staring at me. "Holy Mary," she said, "what happened?"

I sat up and looked down at Teresa and at my own body. We were swollen and bruised, but Teresa slept peacefully on her back, one arm thrown over her head, as Oscar often slept.

The young woman repeated, "What happened? My name is Estela. We heard you crying last night."

As I slowly told our story, Teresa began to whimper, and I held her against me. The woman examined Teresa's cut and bruised arm. "Come inside," she said. I followed her into the tin shack. "This is my husband, Gilberto." She nodded toward a man and at a thin, sickly-looking boy. "That is our son, Juan. It is for his sake that we've got to cross. He keeps getting sicker. It's our only hope. We already lost our little girl." The woman shook her head, moving her long, dark braid. "Here, I've got water and soap. We'll wash the baby's cuts."

Teresa screamed from the burn of the soap, but I held out her arm firmly. Estela glanced over at Gilberto as she worked. "They tried to wade across last night and almost drowned. I don't think we can do that, Gilberto. See how dangerous it is!"

"Why didn't you go with a *coyote?*" Gilberto asked me.

"Because I've just got a little money, and Teresa and

I need to get to Chicago to be with my sister. Besides, last time, when we traveled with *coyotes,* we almost died." Estela crossed herself.

"Yes," she said. "That's the way with us. I also lost a sister and a nephew with *coyotes.* And another sister from bandits. Besides, we only have a little money. But Gilberto has a map."

"My map!" I said out loud. "Tomás's map! I lost it with the food and water."

Estela shook her head. "You lost your map in the river? How sad."

"Thank God we have ours." Gilberto sighed. "If we can get across, the map'll get us to San Antonio."

Estela broke a roll in half and gave part to Teresa and part to me. Little Juan began to cry, and she moved over to him and held him in her arms. "A fever," she said. "It comes and goes." I nodded, thinking of Oscar.

"We can't try to wade across again," I said. "Do you know of any other way?"

Estela nodded. "There is a man who has a rubber raft. He'll take you across to the other bank, no farther, but he charges."

"What?"

"Just thirty American dollars, for any number of people, but we have only ten dollars."

I glanced at Juan and took a breath. "If I furnished the other twenty, would you take me with you, using your map?"

Estela turned to Gilberto. "Yes." He nodded.

She smiled. "We could do it; we could all get across."

As my face also warmed with hope, Teresa clapped her hands, babbled, and plopped backward onto her bottom. We all laughed. But I waited until Estela and Gilberto were not watching to take the money out of my hem.

149

That night, an old man led us along the bank of the river until we reached a spot where a young man stood guard over a rubber raft. Again, I carried water and the food I had bought during the day in a bag. We'd given baby aspirin and the other medicine to both Juan and Teresa, and they were quiet. We slid down to the edge of the river, and when I stepped into the water to board the raft, I felt a moment of panic. But then I saw the Guatemalan woman and the quetzals in her eyes and felt a little more courageous. I set Teresa down in the raft, climbed into it next to her, and held her against me. The young man pushed the raft into the river, and the old man began to paddle us all across, the water barely lapping as he moved the oar in the near dark. No one spoke.

The stars were bright as I watched them. Soon it would be a year since we lost Papá and Ramón and began our long travels. Papá, I thought, searching the sky. Where in the stars are you? Mamá, have you seen him? Then, hearing the churning of the whirlpools, I looked down, picturing the old woman climbing the mountain in my dream. When I glanced up, the other bank was blocking out the stars.

The old man whispered, "Climb out now, and be quiet. May God be with you." I stepped into the shallow water and lifted Teresa and my bag out of the raft. Gilberto carried Juan, and all of us climbed up the bank, where we lay in the grass as we listened for *la migra*. Teresa whimpered and I put my hand over her mouth. I heard night birds.

Finally, Gilberto whispered, "Let's go. Stay close to me." We walked quickly through the dark, stumbling at times. Gilberto occasionally lit a match and looked at the map. Estela carried Teresa for awhile, but Teresa began to fuss so Estela gave her back to me. I tied her on my hip again, and she quieted down. In the distance, I heard a dog bark.

Suddenly, a purring sound came from the sky. I stared up toward the stars as it grew louder. "A helicopter! Fall down!" Estela cried. I threw Teresa and my bag onto the ground, hearing my water bottle break in the process. I lay down on top of Teresa and held her against me. She thrashed and began to cry, and again I put my hand over her mouth. She fought and twisted her body, but I held her tightly.

The helicopter grew louder and louder, and I saw a blue light sweeping the ground. I pressed us against the earth and thought I heard Julia scream. But the light swept past us and continued on. The crashing sound of the motor kept echoing in my ears, and I lay against Teresa and the earth, praying. Finally, the sound dimmed, and I heard Gilberto repeating the "Our Father." Juan and Estela were crying quietly. "They didn't see us," Gilberto whispered. "God wants us to survive. Too bad you lost your water, María. Now we'll have to share."

After we waded across an irrigation ditch in the near dark, Gilberto said quietly, "Let's spend the rest of the night here. I think it's too dangerous to go on because of snakes. We couldn't see them." As I tried to smooth out the ground for Teresa and me to lie on, Gilberto continued, "We'll drink the rest of our water tonight, and in the morning I'll go looking for more. I'll try to make people think I work in the fields around here." Teresa quieted instantly when we lay down. I watched the stars, and Estela sang softly to Juan.

I heard a dog barking and awoke early the next morning. I didn't move but lay on my side, blinking at the light. Teresa was sleeping against my legs, and Gilberto and

Estela were lying next to each other, up and to my left. I noticed Juan. He stood away from us, rubbing his fist against his eye, silhouetted against the dawn. Then I heard the rattling. "Juan!" I cried, and he turned toward us. Estela and Gilberto jumped up, startled out of sleep, and the snake slithered away into the dry brush.

Estela cradled Juan in her arms. "I hate this. I hate having to go through this," she cried.

A short time later, Gilberto left to search for water. When he returned with it, we drank and walked again, stumbling through much of the day with heat and exhaustion. Finally, we stopped by some rocks to rest. Estela sat down, put Juan's head on her lap, and held some water to his lips. She felt his forehead. "Oh, Our Lady, he's hot. Feel him, María." I touched his face. He reminded me so much of Oscar.

Gilberto knelt down and also felt Juan's forehead. "He's really sick," Gilberto said. "According to the map, we must be somewhere near Edinburg. Maybe there's a doctor there, or maybe I could find work so we could take the bus to San Antonio. If we could get to the city, our aunt could heal him."

I watched and thought of the money I still had. Then I pictured Julia and what she'd almost had to do to get the money for us, and I pictured what Doña Elena had sold. I swallowed. "I still have money," I said. "Maybe enough for a bus to get us to San Antonio, if it is safe to go to town. Would you help me find work in San Antonio so I could get the money to go to Chicago?"

Estela stared at me, her braid over one shoulder. "Oh, you're a blessing to us, María."

I glanced down and over at Gilberto. His eyes were lowered and I thought I saw tears. I turned quickly away, so as not to hurt his pride. "Yes, a blessing," he said quietly.

So the next morning, we walked slowly to the edge of the town. I left Teresa with the others in a thicket in a vacant lot, quietly entered a store, and asked in English, "Pampers? I buy Pampers?" Returning to them, I dressed Teresa for the United States. We walked out onto the sidewalks, like the other people, and no one seemed to notice us. Finally, we came to a building marked BUS DEPOT.

I opened the door to the building. Cool air struck my face and I smelled disinfectant. We stepped inside. People sat on benches, and a man stood behind a ticket window. I turned to Gilberto and said quietly. "Sit down. I'll take Teresa into the bathroom and get out my money." Estela took Juan from Gilberto's arms, and they all sat on the bench. I carried Teresa across the room and through a door marked LADIES.

An old black woman was bent over a mop in the bathroom, scrubbing the floor and singing as she worked. She glanced up at me and blinked her eyes, and I thought of the Quetzal Lady. "God," she said in English, then slowly, "You look bad, girl."

I stared back at her, not knowing what to say, and set Teresa down by the sink. Teresa grabbed my legs and cried, gazing with fear at the woman. I took some paper towels, wet them, and bent down and washed Teresa's face.

The old woman went back to her singing and mopping, and I took Teresa with me into a toilet, stuck my hand down inside my dress, and took out the rest of the money. I understood a few words from the woman's song, "River . . . chilly and wide. . . ." I heard the slop of the wet mop on the floor. ". . . but friends . . . on other side . . ." I stepped outside the toilet, holding Teresa on my hip, and I saw myself in the mirror. I was as dark and thin as a shadow, but we were alive. I glanced

153

over and saw the reflection of the old woman, staring at me and still singing. I crossed the wet floor, opened the door to the main room, and saw them.

A uniformed border patrolman was putting handcuffs on Gilberto, and another man in a uniform held Estela by one elbow. Juan was crying in Estela's arms, and she glanced up at me. Our eyes met for a second, and she turned away. I pulled back into the bathroom, shaking as I held Teresa, and the old black woman looked up at me and smiled, showing me a sign. "CLOSED FOR CLEANING," she said and pointed to it. She pushed the bucket and mop out of the room and closed the door behind her. I heard her hang the sign on the bathroom door. I held Teresa in the bathroom and cried.

I cried for Estela, Gilberto, and Juan and because I finally knew. My saving Teresa wouldn't bring Papá back or always keep Oscar strong. It would have nothing to do with determining when we'd be together with Mamá. I cried and cried, sitting on the floor, holding Teresa as she whimpered in my arms. Finally, I calmed. We did have Teresa. Little Teresa. And Mamá was alive. I rocked Teresa slowly in my arms.

Late that afternoon, Teresa and I were on the bus going north. First we would go to San Antonio and then on to Chicago. We stopped at an Immigration checkpoint shortly after the trip began, but when a border patrolman climbed on the bus, he just glanced at my identification, then motioned the driver to continue northward. "Thank God, we can relax. We've passed the last checkpoint," I heard a man say in Spanish.

I looked across the fields. The sun was low in the sky and etched the crops and workers with light. Hawks flew high above them. I thought of the cold and grayness of Chicago but also pictured Julia, Oscar, baby Ramona, Tomás, Doña Elena, and the others. I saw tears in Julia's eyes as she greeted us and felt Julia and me lying awake on our mattress, talking as the little ones slept against us. Then I saw Oscar, balanced mostly on one foot, standing wrapped in his coat and in the old curtain, Tomás standing behind him. "Papá, I wish you were with us. Mamá, come to us soon." I closed my eyes.

A few minutes later, I felt a light patting on my cheek. Teresa stood on my lap, her eyes blinking. "Tesa, Tesa, Tesa," she said. *"Mi'a, Mi'a."* She laughed.

I watched her and thought of the words on the wall of Ana's church in Onarga. "For the child shall die a hundred years old," I whispered. Then, smiling at my baby sister, I began my story. "In a warm village with a thousand colors, there lived a little sparrow who loved a little girl."